WhaT They're Saying AbouT

"Ramona is one of the
funniest little sisters in fiction."
—*New York Times*
★ ON BEEZUS AND RAMONA ★

"True, warm-hearted, and funny."
—ALA *Booklist* (STARRED REVIEW)
★ ON RAMONA AND HER FATHER ★

"It's a rare thing to be hailed
by audience and critics alike.
In Mrs. Cleary's case,
everyone seems delighted."
—*New York Times*
★ ON RAMONA QUIMBY, AGE 8 ★

"Hooray for Beverly Cleary!
Bravo for RAMONA THE BRAVE!"
—*Reading Teacher*
★ ON RAMONA THE BRAVE ★

Ramona's World

Beverly Cleary

Illustrated by Alan Tiegreen

SCHOLASTIC INC.
New York Toronto London Auckland Sydney
Mexico City New Delhi Hong Kong Buenos Aires

ISBN-13: 978-0-439-21963-1
ISBN-10: 0-439-21963-9

36 35 34   12/0

Printed in the U.S.A.   40

This edition first printing, September 2007

Contents

❖ 1 ❖
Ramona Spreads the News

Ramona Quimby was nine years old. She had brown hair, brown eyes, and no cavities. She had a mother, a father, a big sister named Beatrice who was called Beezus by the family, and—this was the exciting part—a baby sister named Roberta after her father, Robert Quimby.

"Look at her tiny fingernails," Ramona marveled as she looked at the sleeping Roberta, "and her little eyebrows. She is already a whole person, only little." Ramona couldn't wait for the first day of school so she could spread the news about her baby sister.

That day finally came. It was a warm September day, and Ramona, neat and clean, with lunch bag in hand, half skipped, half hopped, scrunching through dry leaves on the sidewalk. She was early, she knew, but Ramona was the sort of girl who was always early because something might happen that she didn't want to miss. The fourth grade was going to be the best year of her life, so far.

Ramona was first to arrive at the bus stop in front of Mrs. Pitt's house. Mrs. Pitt came out the front door and began sweeping her front steps.

"Hi, Mrs. Pitt," Ramona called out. "Guess what! My baby sister is two months old."

"Good for her," said Mrs. Pitt, agreeable to a baby in the neighborhood. Babies did not scatter candy wrappers or old spelling papers on the lawn in front of her house.

Ramona pretended she was playing hopscotch until her friend Howie, who was already familiar

with Roberta, joined her along with other children, some with their mothers, who were excited about the first day of school. "Hi, Ramona," he said, and leaned against a tree in the strip of grass between the sidewalk and the street. He opened his lunch bag and began to eat his sandwich. Ramona knew he was doing this so he wouldn't be bothered carrying his lunch.

"Little boy!" Mrs. Pitt called out. "Little boy, don't you drop any papers or orange peels in front of my house. And stay off my grass!"

"Okay." Howie took another bite of his sandwich as he moved to the sidewalk. Howie was not easily excited, which Ramona sometimes found annoying. She was often excited. She *liked* to be excited.

When the yellow bus stopped, Ramona was first on board. She plunked herself down on a seat across the aisle from another fourth grader, a boy named Danny who was wearing a white T-shirt with *Trail Blazers* printed on it. Ramona called him Yard Ape because she thought he acted like an ape on the playground. She was glad he had not moved away during the summer. "I have a new baby sister," she informed him.

Yard Ape closed his eyes and hit his forehead with the palm of his hand. "Another Ramona," he said, and groaned.

Ramona refused to smile. "You have a little brother," she reminded him.

"I know," answered Yard Ape, "but we just keep him for a pet."

Ramona made a face at him so he wouldn't know she liked him.

When Ramona jumped off the bus at Cedarhurst School, she greeted old friends, most of them in new, or at least clean, clothes for starting the fourth grade. When she saw Janet, whom she had often seen in the park during the summer, the two girls compared calluses on the palms of their hands. "Your calluses are really big," said Janet, impressed.

It was true. Ramona's calluses were hard and yellow because she lived close to the park, where she often went with Beezus and her mother and Roberta on warm summer days. She worked hard at the rings—*pump, pump, swing, pump, pump, swing*—and by the end of summer she was able to travel down the line of rings and back again.

"There's Susan," cried Janet, and ran to join her. Reluctantly Ramona followed. "Hi, Susan," she said, eyeing Susan's short blond curls.

"Hi, Ramona," answered Susan. Neither girl smiled. The trouble was the grown-up Quimbys and Susan's parents, the Kushners, were friends. Ramona did not know what Mrs. Kushner said, but her own parents often said things like, "Now, you be nice to Susan," "Susan is such a well-behaved little girl," or "Susan's mother says Susan always sets the table without being asked." Such remarks did not endear Susan to Ramona. There was more. In kindergarten Susan did not like Ramona, who could not resist pulling the long curls she had at that time and saying, *"Boing!"* as she released them. In first grade, when the class was making owls out of paper bags, Susan copied Ramona's owl. The teacher held up Susan's owl to show the class what a splendid owl Susan had made. This seemed so unfair to Ramona that she crunched Susan's owl and found herself in trouble, big trouble. So how could anyone expect the two girls to be friends? As Ramona expected, the calluses on Susan's hands were so small they could scarcely be seen.

Then Ramona saw a new girl who was standing alone. A new fourth grader, Ramona decided, and because she admired the girl's long fair hair she went over to her and asked, "What's your name?"

"Daisy," answered the girl. "Daisy Kidd." When she smiled, Ramona saw that she was wearing bands on her teeth. "What's your name?" Daisy asked. As Ramona told her, the bell rang, ending their conversation.

On her way to the fourth grade Ramona passed her former classroom, where the teacher was standing outside the door welcoming her new class. When she saw Ramona, she waved and said, "How's bright-eyed, bushy-tailed Ramona?"

People often called Ramona bright-eyed and bushy-tailed. When she was younger, she blinked her eyes, held up her hands like paws, and wiggled her bottom as if she were wagging a tail. Now that she was a fourth grader, she was too grown-up for such babyishness, so she waved and said, "Hi, Mrs. Whaley."

Ramona's fourth-grade teacher was Mrs. Meacham, a plump, cheerful woman in a green pantsuit and blouse printed with flowers, a good sign. Ramona liked teachers who wore bright cheerful clothes. Mrs. Meacham, Ramona decided, must be very old, because Howie's father had gone to school with her when he was a boy.

After inspecting her new teacher, Ramona looked at the chalkboard for spelling words. The board was blank, another good sign. Mrs. Meacham passed out name tags and made a little speech about how learning was fun in the fourth grade and everyone should work together to make this a great year. She then passed out papers with borders of dinosaurs, another hopeful sign,

Ramona thought, even though dinosaurs were more for third graders than fourth graders. Mrs. Meacham said, "So I will get to know you better, I want each of you to write a paragraph telling me about yourself."

Ramona tapped her pencil on her nose and noticed that Yard Ape, who sat across the aisle, was already writing, apparently without having to think. Susan, in front of Ramona, leaned her head on her fist. A boy went to the pencil sharpener. Someone sighed. Feet shuffled. Ramona began to write. She enjoyed writing in cursive because her third-grade teacher once said, "Ramona, your cursive is better than mine." Now she wrote fast because she had so much to say: "My name is Ramona Quimby. I have a baby sister. She is cute. She screems if she is hunrgy." Ramona paused. *Screems* looked peculiar. Maybe it was spelled with *ea* instead of *ee*. Oh, well. Anyone would know what she meant. She had so much to say she did not want to waste time spelling. "Sometimes I sit on the coach and hold her."

Ramona enjoyed writing. Her face grew flushed as she wrote faster and faster toward the dinosaurs at the bottom of the page. Her last lines, not as neat as her first, were written across the dinosaur heads. "She can grab my figner. Mother says I used to look like her. She says I can be her roll modle." Ramona squeezed a tiny sketch of a baby's sleeping face between a brontosaurus and a tyrannosaurus.

Ramona was proud of her work. She glanced around to see what her classmates had written about themselves. She leaned forward to look over Susan's shoulder. Susan had written half a page in neat cursive and was busy coloring dinosaurs, neatly of course, with crayons. Ramona read, "My name is Susan. My favorite color is blue. My favorite food is . . ." Ramona did not need to read any further. She half rose from her seat to look across the aisle toward Yard Ape and read in his neat uphill cursive, "My name is Daniel. Call me Yard Ape. I am nine years old. I am not married. I am a kid and proud of it."

Me too, thought Ramona, filled with admiration for Yard Ape, a smart boy who always earned stars or Good Work! at the top of his papers and looked as if he was about to get into trouble. Somehow he never did, not in the classroom. On the playground he ran faster, yelled louder, and kicked balls farther than any of the other boys.

"All right, class," said Mrs. Meacham, "pass your papers to the front." Ramona was so pleased with her work she was almost sorry to part with it.

At lunchtime when the class went to the multipurpose room, Daisy sat down beside Ramona. "Okay if I sit here?" she asked.

"Sure," said Ramona. Together the girls tore open their lunch bags. They shared Ramona's corn chips and each ate half of Daisy's brownie. Ramona told Daisy about Roberta; Daisy wished she had a little sister. She only had a big brother. Ramona admired Daisy's long blond hair; Daisy admired Ramona's short hair and said she was lucky to have hair that didn't get tangled when it was washed. It was a good beginning.

After lunch Mrs. Meacham said, "I've had time to look over what you have written. There is one description I would like to read to you."

Mine! Mine! Ramona silently prayed, and sure enough, it was Ramona's description of Roberta that her teacher chose to read. Mrs. Meacham did not seem to notice a few misspelled words, because she knew what Ramona meant. The class seemed to enjoy it, and Ramona was ecstatic. She couldn't wait to tell her mother.

The rest of the day passed quickly. Ramona ran

all the way home from the bus and found her mother sitting on the couch drinking tea and reading a book for her book club, which met once a month. "Guess what!" Ramona burst out. "I wrote a composition about Roberta."

"Sh-h-h. Roberta's asleep." Mrs. Quimby placed a marker in her book and closed it. "Sounds interesting," she said, and took a sip of tea.

"It was," whispered Ramona. "It was so interesting that Mrs. Meacham read it to the whole class. Mrs. Meacham is about a million years old, but she's nice."

"I can't wait to read your composition," said her mother.

Ramona frowned thoughtfully. "I suppose I could have said Roberta spits up sometimes."

"We don't have to tell the whole world our little secrets." Mrs. Quimby looked amused, which Ramona found pleasant, not like being laughed at. Mrs. Quimby sipped her tea.

It was a moment for confidences. Ramona told her mother, "There's a new girl named Daisy Kidd with bands on her teeth and long golden hair like a fairy princess and a brownie in her lunch. I know I am going to like her a lot."

"Good. She sounds nice," said Mrs. Quimby.

Ramona picked up her mother's book. *Moby Dick.* "What's this about?" she asked.

"A whale that bit off a man's leg," said Mrs. Quimby. "Our book club decided to read a book we had all heard about all our lives but had never actually read."

"Sounds exciting." Ramona opened the book, which turned out not to look exciting at all. The print was small, the lines were close together, and there were almost no quotation marks. She closed the book. She liked her own writing better. That wasn't all she liked. She liked Mrs. Meacham, she liked Daisy, she liked Yard Ape, she liked the fourth grade. It was going to be a great year.

✦ 2 ✦
The Role Model

The next morning Ramona was excited and happy when she entered her classroom, that is, until she saw—she might have known—spelling words on the chalkboard. She mentally groaned. Why did nice Mrs. Meacham have to do this? She soon found out.

Mrs. Meacham explained. "Today we are going to study words we use. When we wrote about ourselves, we discovered words we need to learn how to spell."

Ramona looked more closely at the words on the chalkboard. Among them she saw *scream, hungry, couch, finger, role, model.* They looked familiar. They were familiar. They were her words. She scowled.

"Is something the matter, Ramona?" asked Mrs. Meacham, who had been quick to learn names.

Ramona decided to speak up. "What difference does spelling make if people know what you mean?" she asked.

"You wouldn't want people to think you sat on a coach instead of a couch, would you?" Mrs. Meacham asked.

The class found this funny, but Ramona did not, not when the class laughed. She felt her face grow hot. She slid down in her seat and shook her head. Mrs. Meacham knew the answer. Why did she bother to ask?

Mrs. Meacham continued, "And before lunch are you hungry or hunrgy?"

The class laughed, harder this time. The warm day suddenly seemed warmer. Ramona decided

right then that she *did not like Mrs. Meacham,* and this was only the second day of school. Mrs. Meacham did not tell the truth. She said learning was fun, and it wasn't. At least not all the time. Not when it came to spelling.

The fourth grade suddenly began to stretch ahead, long and dreary and full of spelling. Before long, rain would begin to fall, day after day. The school bus would smell like old boots. Then, with luck, snow might fall. Ramona imagined herself making snow angels in the front yard.

"Ramona, please join the class." Mrs. Meacham spoke sharply. The class laughed a third time.

Ramona sat up and stared glumly at the spelling words on the chalkboard. She did not really want to be a bad speller. She simply did not want to bother being a good speller. She had more interesting things to do, although at the moment she couldn't think what. She frowned and studied the words based on her own misspellings as well as those of others and disliked every minute. Mrs. Meacham gave a little talk on not confusing *h* with *k* in cursive writing and pointed to *muck* on the chalkboard. Ramona knew *much* was not her word but that of some babyish person in the class. Imagine spelling it *muck*. How silly.

When recess came, Yard Ape stopped chasing a ball to ask, "What kind of coach did you sit on? Baseball or football?"

"You keep quiet." Ramona saw no reason to be polite, especially when the day was so warm. Then she had an inspiration. "I sat on a coach like a stagecoach," she informed him. She could tell he didn't believe her.

Susan smiled that superior smile of hers and said nothing.

"Everybody makes mistakes," Janet reminded Ramona.

"I'm a rotten speller, too," said Howie, as if that would help.

Daisy smiled, showing the bands on her teeth, and said, "I don't think Mrs. Meacham was very nice to you." Ramona felt better.

When the long day finally ended, Ramona sat as far as she could from Yard Ape on the bus. She gave ever-sweeping Mrs. Pitt a tiny smile and did not bother to wave. At home she found her mother sitting on the couch, not coach, still reading *Moby Dick*.

"Sh-h-h," said Mrs. Quimby. "Don't wake Roberta. She was fussy last night and the heat makes her cross." She laid her book aside. "What happened in school today?"

Ramona was in no mood to be hushed. "Oh— nothing much. Same old stuff. Spelling and multiplication facts and stuff." Then, because her mother often told her to look on the bright side, she added, "Daisy gave me half of her chocolate-chip cookie."

"That's good." Mrs. Quimby spoke as if she was thinking of something else. "Ramona," she said in that quiet voice that meant Ramona was about to get a little talking-to, "you've been using the word *stuff* entirely too much. Surely you can find a better word to say what you mean."

Ramona felt picked on, first by her teacher and now by her mother. *Stuff* was a perfectly good, handy, multipurpose word and easy to spell, too. She flopped into a chair and scowled. If she had written, "My sister is cute and stuff," or "I like to hold her and stuff," she wouldn't have misspelled so many words, and Mrs. Meacham wouldn't have had a chance to be so mean.

Before the discussion could continue, Beezus came home from school, dumped an armload of books on the dining room table, and gave her mother and sister a cheerful "Hi."

Ramona returned it with a grumpy "Hi."

Beezus, smiling and full of enthusiasm, perched

on the arm of the couch. "I love high school. I didn't get lost in the halls even once today. I think I made a new friend. My French teacher makes French seem easy, and I have the nicest man teacher for English, and—"

Ramona interrupted. "And I suppose you spelled every single word right."

"Well, aren't you Miss Grouchypuss?" Beezus said. "Yes, I did, and in French, too."

"Smartypuss," countered Ramona, feeling that everyone picked on her.

"Girls!" Mrs. Quimby's voice was weary. The afternoon was too warm for this sort of disagreement. From the bedroom came the sound of fussing, crying, and finally screaming.

S-c-r-e-a-m, thought Ramona, mentally spelling the word in spite of herself.

"I'll get her," Beezus offered.

Good old Beezus, thought Ramona, sliding farther down in the chair.

"Ramona, *please*," said Mrs. Quimby. "Try to be agreeable."

"I am agreeable," said Ramona with an even darker scowl.

Beezus returned with sobbing Roberta in her arms. Because of the heat the baby was wearing only a diaper. "What's the matter with Roberta?" Beezus crooned, and kissed the baby's hair.

Mrs. Quimby held out her arms for Roberta, who snuggled against her mother's shoulder. "Sh-h-h," whispered her mother. Roberta stopped crying with one last hiccuping sob. "That's my good girl," whispered Mrs. Quimby, and she too kissed the baby's hair.

All this made Ramona feel worse than ever—unloved, left out, and a rotten speller with the whole horrible fourth grade ahead of her. Nobody kissed her hair, at least today, and it was clean, too. She pulled herself out of the chair, found the remote control, and turned on the television to a rerun of her favorite after-school program, *Big Hospital.* She wanted to forget her troubles and lose herself in the corridors of the hospital where people in green pajamas fell in love if they weren't

too busy saving lives or comforting the lost and lonely.

"Ramona, please turn that off." Mrs. Quimby looked over Roberta's head at her middle daughter. "I wish you'd tell me what's bothering you."

"Nothing's bothering me," grumped Ramona as she pushed the button on the remote control without finding out what Handsome Doctor and Blond Nurse would say next. She waited for her mother to coax her problems out of her, to soothe her, to tell her things would be better tomorrow, and maybe even kiss her hair. She picked at a callus but did not pull it off. Calluses were one thing she had to be proud of. Right now she felt they were the only thing.

Before Mrs. Quimby could coax, the telephone rang. "I'll get it!" Beezus shouted. She and Ramona usually tried to beat each other to the telephone in the hall.

Of course, Ramona eavesdropped. She heard Beezus say, sounding surprised, "Yes, I'd love to, but I'll have to ask Mother. Just a minute—"

Beezus, her eyes shining and her face alight with joy, came back into the room and said, "Mother, guess what! Mrs. Lucas wants me to baby-sit with Benjamin Saturday evening. They won't be out late, and they'll pay me and everything!"

And stuff, thought Ramona.

Beezus continued. "And Mrs. Lucas says she wants me because she knows I'm responsible. Oh, please, *please*—"

"I don't see why not," said Mrs. Quimby. "We'll be home, so we could help if there is an emergency, which I'm sure there won't be."

Not with good old Beezus being so responsible all over the place, thought Ramona as Beezus danced off to the telephone. After she had accepted the offer, she returned, gathered up her books, and started down the hall to the room the sisters had shared since Roberta was born. The baby now occupied Ramona's old room.

Beezus paused and said, *"Au revoir."*

"What does that mean?" asked Ramona,

annoyed with Beezus for using words she did not understand.

"It means goodbye in French," answered Beezus, and went off to the room the sisters shared. Probably to be responsible about her homework, thought Ramona.

Mrs. Quimby shifted Roberta to her lap and patted the couch beside her. "Ramona, come sit by me," she coaxed.

Reluctantly Ramona moved to the couch, staying as far away as she could from her mother. She balanced the heel of one sandal on the toe of the other and longed to lean against her mother and confide her troubles. Life was hard enough, and now Beezus would be showing off by speaking French. She picked at a callus.

"Can you tell me what's bothering you?" Mrs. Quimby's voice was gentle. Roberta stared at Ramona as if she were giving her serious thought.

"Nothing." Ramona sighed.

"Now, Ramona," her mother said in her soothing voice, "I know something's bothering you. You'll feel better if you tell me."

Ramona knew her mother was right, but she sighed again before she burst out, "My spelling is rotten and Mrs. Meacham doesn't like me and makes me feel stupid in front of the whole class and they laughed at me and made me feel super-stupid and everybody says Beezus is responsible and nobody says I'm responsible and everybody fusses over Roberta and says she is cute and adorable and stuff and nobody pays any attention to me and I'm not supposed to say 'stuff' and— and—stuff."

Roberta looked worried.

Mrs. Quimby ignored the stuffs. "Has anybody ever said you weren't responsible?" she asked.

Ramona thought. "Well—no," she admitted, "but Mrs. Meacham probably will. She only likes people who can spell. She *loves* good spellers. She *adores* good spellers."

Mrs. Quimby smiled. "Ramona, I think you are exaggerating."

Ramona knew her mother was right, but that was the way she felt. Exaggerating felt *good*.

"Bring your spelling words home, and we'll help

you." Mrs. Quimby was comforting, but Ramona was not ready to be comforted. "And don't forget," her mother went on, "this is only the second day of school, and Mrs. Meacham is there to teach you. You'll feel differently when you get to know her better and when your spelling improves."

Ramona felt calmer after spilling out her troubles, but she wasn't ready to admit it. How did she know her spelling would improve? It might get worse. Roberta stared as if she were trying to understand. Ramona stared back, still engulfed in self-pity, and thought, I wish somebody would call me darling and adorable like Roberta. But no, I'm just plain old messy Ramona. She stuck her tongue out at Roberta and immediately felt ashamed of herself. Her sweet innocent baby sister—

Then, to Ramona's astonishment, Roberta stuck her tongue out at Ramona. Ramona couldn't believe it. Roberta was too little to understand. It must have been a coincidence. As an experiment Ramona stuck *her* tongue out again. Roberta smiled a real smile and stuck *her* tongue out again.

It was a game. Ramona could scarcely believe what she had seen. "Mother, did you see that?" she asked in wonder. "Roberta stuck her tongue out when I stuck my tongue out, and she smiled, really smiled, like it was some kind of game."

Mrs. Quimby laughed. "I told you Roberta would take after you."

"But she's so awfully little," said Ramona, still marveling.

"Babies are more observant than we realize," said Mrs. Quimby.

Ramona's troubles seemed to vanish. She had taught her baby sister to stick out her tongue. She could teach her other things when she was older, things like playing tic-tac-toe and roller-skating. As for spelling—pooh! Mrs. Meacham was just another teacher. Ramona had survived others, liked them, and even loved her kindergarten teacher. She would survive Mrs. Meacham, maybe get to like her, even though at the moment this seemed doubtful. Ramona didn't care. Suddenly the sun was shining—it had shone all day, but Ramona hadn't noticed, since she had gone to school—and now Roberta had copied her by sticking out her tongue.

Ramona felt so good she held up her finger to Roberta, who grasped it in her tiny perfect hand. "See," Ramona said to her mother, "I really am Roberta's role model." Then, in spite of herself, Ramona thought, *r-o-l-e m-o-d-e-l.*

✦ 3 ✦
At Daisy's House

As September sunshine changed to autumn clouds, life at the Quimbys' house settled into a peaceful routine. Mr. Quimby, who managed the Shop-rite Market, came home from work looking cheerful. Groceries had been delivered on time, no shoplifters were spotted, and no one had slipped on bits of lettuce dropped by careless produce customers.

Mrs. Quimby found more time to read *Moby Dick*, a book with so many pages that members of the book club, most of them mothers or women who worked outside their homes or both, had difficulty finishing it. They postponed their meeting for another month. Ramona wondered why they didn't just skip the hard parts.

Roberta was a happy baby, busy enjoying her hands and feet. She could even put her toes in her mouth. So could Ramona, just barely, but no one else in the family even tried.

Beezus was still filled with enthusiasm for high school. She liked all her teachers, and she had made a new friend, Abby Alexander, whose real name was Abigail. At dinnertime the Quimbys heard a lot about Abby: Abby wanted to be a math teacher or a dietician someday, Abby's mother got her contact lenses, Abby got an A on her math test, Abby this and Abby that.

All this left Ramona full of wishes. She sighed a lot and wished she had long hair like Daisy, and even though she had no need for them she wished she had bands on her teeth. She unfolded a paper clip, held the wire in front of her mouth, and smiled at herself in the mirror to see what she

would look like if she wore bands. She wished she
were a better speller without having to work at it,
she wished Yard Ape would pay as much attention
to her in school as on the bus, but most of all she
wished there were girls her age on Klickitat Street.
She wanted girls to play with. She wanted a best

friend. That was why she ran all the way home from the bus stop one afternoon. She had news. A wish might be about to come true.

"Guess what!" she cried as she burst through the door and found her mother folding diapers on the living room couch. They were diapers Ramona had worn, but she didn't like to think about that. Paper diapers were expensive, she knew.

"What am I to guess?" Mrs. Quimby was interested but not excited. After all, she had known Ramona for nine years.

Ramona was glad Roberta was still napping, so she could have her mother all to herself. She took a deep breath and began, "Daisy Kidd, the new girl in my class I told you about—you know, the one with long hair and braces on her teeth—wants me to come home with her on the bus after school tomorrow! Her mother will bring me home after dinner."

Mrs. Quimby pulled a diaper out of the jumble beside her and flapped it to shake out the wrinkles, but before she could answer, Ramona went on, "Please, please, Mother. I never get to play with a girl because there aren't any girls around here except Willa Jean, who doesn't count because she is only in kindergarten and besides, she's a nuisance, and Daisy is lots of fun and she's a good speller and is a really, really nice girl, so she must have really, really nice parents and—"

Mrs. Quimby calmly folded the diaper as she interrupted. "Of course you may go, dear. I already know about Daisy's family because one of the book club members' cousins lives next door to her family and says they are fine people. Daisy's father was transferred here during the summer, and her mother works mornings as a school nurse." Obviously the conversation of the book club was not limited to books.

Somehow Ramona felt let down. She had expected to argue, to have to persuade her mother of the niceness of Daisy and the importance of their playing together.

"You could have asked Daisy to come here," Mrs. Quimby said.

"Oh. I didn't think about it," admitted Ramona. "I guess because we ride different buses."

Mrs. Quimby laid down the diaper she was folding to look thoughtfully at Ramona before she said, "Don't you think you should play with Susan once in a while?"

Ramona picked at the one callus that had not peeled off since school started before she said, "Do I have to? I see her at Sunday school."

Mrs. Quimby said, "You could ask her to come here or you could go to Susan's house. Her mother was saying just the other day that you girls should get together more often."

Ramona made a face. She wished grown-ups would stay out of their children's affairs.

Mrs. Quimby was curious. "Don't you like Susan?" she asked.

"Well—not really," confessed Ramona. "She's the kind of girl who gets mad, really mad, when boys call her Snoozin' Susan. When boys call you a name, you are just supposed to get a little bit mad and not go telling the teacher." Ramona found her reason for disliking Susan difficult to explain. "And I don't like to go to her house because—well, it is too clean, I guess."

Mrs. Quimby looked surprised. "You can't say that about our house."

Ramona was loyal to her house. "Our house isn't dirty," she said. "There are magazines and stu— things on the coffee table, but everything isn't all nicey-nice and just so, and you don't hang around talking when someone comes over. You mind your own business."

"Thank you, dear." Mrs. Quimby's mouth was serious, but her eyes were smiling. "I'm glad to know."

The evening could not pass fast enough for Ramona. The next afternoon she was filled with excitement as she climbed with Daisy onto the bus. After showing her permission note to the driver, the girls found seats together. Ramona felt as if she were about to have an adventure. Although she was familiar with the streets they rode through, somehow they seemed different when seen from someone else's school bus. "I feel like I'm really going someplace," she told Daisy. She had never been so far from home without an adult before.

"You are going someplace," said Daisy. "To my house." Both girls found this funny.

Daisy's house turned out to be an old two-story house on the other side of the high school. The girls were greeted by a friendly tail-wagging dog, a sort of collie. Daisy patted and introduced him. "This is Mutley. My brother Jeremy found him abandoned in the park."

"Hi, Mutley," said Ramona. The dog seemed pleased.

Daisy's house had a pleasant fragrance, something like cookies, and was comfortably untidy. There were still packing boxes in the corner of the living room, and a vacuum cleaner and its attachments lay nearby. A cat dozed in a patch of sunlight and opened one eye to look at Ramona.

Daisy's mother, who was plump, looked younger than her hair, which was gray, long, and held back with a clasp. "Welcome, Ramona," she said as she looked up from a box filled with dishes, crumpled newspaper, and bubble wrap. "What nice shoes you're wearing."

Ramona looked down at her shoes, surprised by their niceness.

Mrs. Kidd continued, "Daisy needs new shoes, but we're not familiar with stores around here. Where do you buy your shoes?"

Ramona knew right away that she liked Mrs. Kidd. Not every mother who asked questions really wanted to know the answer. Mrs. Kidd plainly was not a person who asked children how they liked school or what they wanted to be when they grew up. "Fix yourselves a snack," she said, and pulled a platter out of a carton. "I hope I can get all these packing boxes out of the living room before Daisy goes to high school." Obviously she was a mother who knew how to mind her own business.

Daisy picked up the large, limp cat that was almost too heavy for her. "This is Clawed," she said. "*C-l-a-w-e-d*," she spelled. "Not like a man's name. My brother named him Clawed because he had been clawed by another cat when he found him hiding in a gutter. Daddy says he hopes Jeremy never finds a wounded skunk."

Ramona stroked Clawed's fur. He was such a nice comfortable cat, unlike Picky-picky, the cat the Quimbys had once had. Daisy returned him to his patch of sunshine before she led the way to the kitchen, where she found juice bars in the refrigerator, another good sign, Ramona thought. Susan's mother provided apples or a glass of milk and graham crackers for an after-school snack. While the girls were busy licking their juice bars, Daisy's brother came in the back door, dropped his book bag on the floor, and said, "Hi, Fence Face," to Daisy as he opened the refrigerator. "And you must be the Ramona we've heard too much about." He began to throw together a sandwich.

"That's my brother Germy," said Daisy. "He thinks he's a genius because he's in high school."

"Jeremy," corrected the brother to Ramona and added, "Tinsel Teeth," to his sister. With that he took his sloppy sandwich and a dill pickle into the living room, where he turned on the television to a sports channel.

Daisy made a face. "I wanted to watch *Big Hospital.* That's my favorite program."

49

"Mine too," said Ramona. Sharing a favorite made her feel closer to Daisy.

When the girls had finished their juice bars, Daisy said, "Come on, let's vacuum Clawed. He loves to be vacuumed." Jeremy, who had picked up the cat, was sitting on the couch with his feet on the coffee table. Mrs. Kidd, busy unpacking dishes, did not seem to mind. Daisy seized the vacuum cleaner and pulled it toward Clawed, who jumped off Jeremy's lap as if he expected it. "Here, you do it," Daisy said, and thrust the vacuum cleaner hose at Ramona as she turned on the vacuum cleaner. "He likes the upholstery attachments. I guess you could say he is upholstered in fur."

Clawed did not run as Ramona expected, but stood bracing himself with his chin raised as if he was enjoying the feel of the attachment Ramona was running down his back. "Some cat," said Ramona.

"Here, let me have a turn," said Daisy, taking the vacuum cleaner from Ramona. Clawed rolled over on his back to allow her to vacuum his soft underneath fur. Ramona was amazed. Picky-picky would never have stood for such a thing. She said so.

"Clawed is a smart cat," Daisy explained. "He knows he won't have to scratch fleas if we run the vacuum cleaner over him." When she finished, Clawed went back to his patch of sunshine. The girls entertained themselves by popping bubbles in the bubble wrap while Mrs. Kidd carried cartons to

the basement. Mutley went to the door and whimpered. Jeremy picked up a leash by the front door and took his dog outside.

"Quick!" directed Daisy. "Before he gets back." She seized the remote control and switched the television from the sports channel to *Big Hospital.* "Pretend we've been watching it all along." The girls settled themselves on the couch and tried to look as if they had been there for some time. When Jeremy returned, Daisy looked up from the screen and, pretending to be surprised to see her brother, said, "Oh, hi, Jeremy."

"Okay, Fence Face, you win," said Jeremy, and went thumping up the stairs to his room. Mutley flattened himself, his nose on his paws, in front of the television set. When Daisy was sure the coast was clear and the girls had suppressed their giggles, she went to the refrigerator for a second helping of juice bars.

Ramona and Daisy contentedly licked their juice bars as they watched Handsome Doctor and Blond Nurse and a number of other people in green pajamas save the life of a little boy who had been hit by a car while playing in the street. His weeping mother, holding the ball he had been chasing, watched through a window on the swinging door.

Ramona's thoughts strayed from the hospital to Daisy, her house, and her family. Everything seemed so calm and so comfortable. Even Clawed and Mutley liked each other. Ramona wished she had a big brother who teased her a little bit. On the television Not-quite-so-handsome Doctor who was secretly married to Blond Nurse joined the mother to watch through the window in the swinging door, but Ramona was thinking about Daisy.

Ramona had never had a girl best friend, only Howie, and now that they were in the fourth grade they did not play together as often as they used to. Howie was always banging around with a hammer, building things. Ramona used to enjoy this, too, but lately, as her mother said, she was at loose ends. She was tired of pounding nails with Howie. She wasn't bored exactly. She could always find something to do, but lately something was missing from her life. She wished she were old enough to baby-sit like Beezus, who was busy every weekend. Now she knew what had been missing—a best friend, a girl best friend.

Big Hospital and Ramona's thoughts were interrupted by a commercial for pills to cure aches and pains followed by another for a spray to relieve stuffy noses. Neither girl was interested.

"Let's be best friends." Daisy spoke suddenly, as if she had just thought of it.

"That's what I was thinking." Ramona, who did not usually feel shy, reached out to pet Mutley with her foot.

"I've been sort of—lonesome, I guess you'd call it—starting a new school," confided Daisy.

"I've always wanted a best friend," Ramona admitted. "My neighborhood is mostly boys. They're okay, but—well, you know."

"I know," agreed Daisy. "Boys can be pretty awful, like Danny on the playground."

Ramona was silent. Yard Ape never did anything bad. He was just smart and lively and liked to tease. She did not want anyone, not even her best friend, to know how much she liked him.

The girls watched television in contented silence. Men in green pajamas ran down the hall wheeling a woman groaning in pain. Her faithful dog followed. "Get that dog out of here!" shouted Handsome Doctor. Mutley looked up, startled, saw he wasn't threatened, and laid his nose on his paws again.

Ramona and Daisy smothered their giggles over Mutley's confusion. A spicy fragrance came from the kitchen. Ramona hoped it meant they would have lasagna for dinner. Lasagna would make her day perfect. She couldn't wait to tell her family all about it. Her thoughts drifted to what she would say: Daisy's mother lets her have juice bars after school, Daisy has a big brother who calls her Fence Face, Daisy vacuums the cat. . . . Now Beezus wasn't the only one with a best friend to talk about. Ramona hoped she could be Daisy's best friend forever.

· 4 ·
The Invitation

One chilly day late in October when rain was beginning to clog the gutters with leaves, Ramona came home alone because it was Daisy's day to see her orthodontist to have the bands on her teeth adjusted. She found her mother sitting on the chair holding Roberta to her shoulder and patting her on the back. An almost empty bottle of formula stood on the lamp table. As Ramona pulled off her raincoat, she inspected a small bald spot on the back of Roberta's head, which at first had frightened

Ramona because she thought Roberta was going bald like their father. Mrs. Quimby had explained that many babies wore off their first hair and that it would soon grow back. And it was, to Ramona's relief.

With her inspection out of the way, Ramona said, as if she were making an important announcement, "Boys are just awful."

"How so?" asked her mother as she patted the baby's back.

"A couple of girls wore knit caps—their mothers made them wear them—and the boys grabbed them and threw them into the boys' bathroom." Boys, at this moment, were very much disapproved of by Ramona, who promised herself she would never, never wear a knit cap to school.

"All boys?" Mrs. Quimby had the look of someone trying to hide a smile. "I can't imagine Howie doing such a dreadful thing."

"Well, maybe not Howie." Ramona backed down but soon flared up again. "Mother," she said sternly. "It is not funny. Boys *are* just awful."

"If you say so, dear" was Mrs. Quimby's mild answer. "How was spelling?"

Ramona was a tiny bit annoyed with her mother for not getting upset over the awfulness of boys and for bringing up spelling. "I missed one word, *project*. I spelled it *p-r-o-d-j-e-c-t*, which is the way it sounds."

Discussion of Ramona's spelling came to an end because Beezus returned from school, dumped her armload of books on a chair, waved an envelope, obviously happy with whatever was in it, and said without bothering to take off her rain jacket, "Guess what?"

"I can't imagine," said Mrs. Quimby.

"You won a million dollars," said Ramona, glad to forget her spelling.

"No, silly. Abby is giving a party two weeks from tomorrow. She passed out the invitations today."

"That's nice." Mrs. Quimby was still patting Roberta's back. "I don't think I know where Abby lives."

"In one of those nice big houses the other side of high school," Beezus explained.

"Will her parents be home?" asked Mrs.
Quimby.

"Oh, *Mom!*" Beezus was annoyed even though
she was used to her mother's concern. "Yes, they

will be home and all that stuff. I asked because I know how old-fashioned you are."

Mrs. Quimby said, "Funny, I used to think my parents were old-fashioned, too."

Stuff, thought Ramona. Beezus said "stuff" and Mother didn't say anything. Then, to avoid arguments between her mother and sister, she said, "I hope you don't have to play pin-the-tail-on-the-donkey."

"Of course not, silly. That's a game for little kids." Beezus spoke as if Ramona were still in kindergarten. "Abby is inviting boys and we're going to dance!"

"Wow!" said Ramona. "But you don't know how to dance."

Beezus seemed to wilt. At that moment Roberta startled them with a noise, the sort of noise Mrs. Quimby called a bubble, Beezus and Ramona called a burp, and Mr. Quimby, when he was being funny, a belch, a word his daughters disapproved of because it sounded too ugly for such a sweet baby.

"Good girl," crooned Mrs. Quimby. Roberta's sisters paid no attention. By now they were used to Roberta.

"How can you dance if you don't know how?" persisted Ramona.

"That's what's bothering me," admitted Beezus. "Abby's mother made her take ballroom dancing lessons to help her be popular, and now she's giving this party to get her going on being popular. Maybe Abby can show me."

"Dancing can't be that hard." Ramona tried to cheer Beezus. "I've seen it on TV. Kids just sort of wiggle around and wave their arms."

"Don't worry. Your father will show you how," reassured Mrs. Quimby.

Ramona thought about Howie and Yard Ape. She could not imagine them dancing.

After the party invitation, telephone calls that were not about baby-sitting began to come for Beezus. Of course, Ramona listened to Beezus's half of the conversations, which involved which boys were invited, which boys might actually come, what to wear, and who said what to whose locker partner in the hall at school. Ramona wished she had a locker at school instead of a coat hook at the back of the classroom. Beezus even got to have a padlock on her locker.

On Saturday afternoon Beezus took her baby-sitting money out of the mug on her study table and in spite of drizzling rain set off to meet some friends at the shopping center. *"Au revoir,"* she said as she went out the door.

Ramona was annoyed with her sister for not speaking plain English and for not asking her to come along. She tried to pass the time reading Mother Goose rhymes to Roberta, because their mother had read a book that said babies should be read to as soon as they were born so they would grow up to be good readers. Ramona wasn't sure how this would work, but she enjoyed the rhymes and read with expression and dramatic gestures. Roberta seemed fascinated, especially with "The Three Little Kittens," which Ramona recited over and over until the baby fell asleep and Mrs. Quimby carried her off to her crib.

Not as much time had passed as Ramona hoped. Late in the day, when Mrs. Quimby was still trying to finish *Moby Dick*, Beezus came home carrying a plastic shopping bag and wearing a head scarf tied under her chin.

That's funny, thought Ramona. Beezus always said head scarves were for old ladies or the Queen of England.

"Successful shopping trip?" Mrs. Quimby barely raised her eyes from her book. The book club meeting was not far away.

"Mm-hm." Beezus beckoned Ramona into their room and shut the door.

"Why are you wearing that dumb scarf?" Ramona demanded. "It isn't that wet outside."

"Sh-h-h." Beezus looked worried. "What am I going to say?" she whispered.

"About what?" asked Ramona.

"My ears." Beezus pulled off her scarf. She was wearing a tiny gold ball in the lobe of each ear.

Ramona was so surprised it took her a moment

before she whispered, "Earrings! What will Mommy and Daddy say?"

"That's what's bothering me." Beezus carefully felt her ears as if to make sure her earrings were still there.

"Well . . ." Ramona was dubious. "I'm glad they're your ears, not mine." Then, because she really wanted to know, she asked, "Did it hurt a lot?"

"Just for a minute, but it was scary," admitted Beezus. "They shoot the earrings into your lobes with a thing that looks like a staple gun."

Ramona winced as Beezus picked up her hairbrush and tried to brush her hair over her ears.

At the same time she admired her sister's courage. "Why don't you show Mother and get it over before Daddy comes home." Ramona was eager to find out what would happen. Besides, she couldn't wait to tell Daisy what Beezus had done.

When the girls advanced cautiously into the living room, Mrs. Quimby glanced up from her book, took a second look, and laid the book down. "Why, Beezus—" she said.

Ramona, ashamed of her curiosity, tried to help her sister. "Some girls in kindergarten have their ears pierced. I've even seen babies with teeny little earrings."

Mrs. Quimby paid no attention to Ramona but said, "Beezus, why didn't you ask?"

Beezus looked both unhappy and defiant. "They are my ears, and I used my baby-sitting money. If I asked, you might not let me."

"Yes, but—" began Mrs. Quimby.

Beezus interrupted. "I'm tired of being plain old responsible Beezus. I'm tired of people saying how sensible I am. I want to be glamorous for a change. People are always asking me to do things because they know I will do them right. Well, I want to wear earrings and lipstick and be somebody different. I want to look nice for the party. I want to have fun!"

Ramona was shocked. She had never heard her sister speak this way in her whole life.

"Oh, Beezus—" Mrs. Quimby had tears in her eyes. "I had no idea— You always seemed so contented."

"Not on the inside," said Beezus in despair. "Just on the outside."

"Oh, Beezus—" repeated Mrs. Quimby as if she could not find words to express her sympathy for her daughter.

Roberta seemed to understand that her home at the moment was not as happy as she wanted it to be. First she looked worried. Then she began to whimper.

"Sh-h-h," soothed Mrs. Quimby, trying to distract the baby before she spoke to Beezus. "You are pretty. You have lovely eyes and shining hair."

"Nobody ever says so." Beezus's anger melted, leaving her wilted and tearful. "And sometimes my face breaks out in spots."

"I think you're sort of pretty, even with spots." Ramona, loyal to her sister, wanted her to be happy. If Beezus was happy, Ramona could look forward to being happy when she reached high school. Not that Ramona wasn't happy now. She was, except sometimes.

Beezus did not seem comforted. She sniffed and blew her nose. "I'm sorry for being such a—I don't know what."

"Don't be." Mrs. Quimby wiped her own eyes. "Everyone has to let off a little steam now and then. I'm glad to know how you feel. I don't know what your father will say, but cheer up. What's done is done. Next Saturday we'll go shopping for some pretty earrings and something to wear to the party."

"Thank you," said Beezus with a watery smile as her mother carried Roberta off to the bedroom to change her.

"One down, one to go," said Ramona as if life were a football game on television. Beezus picked up a magazine and sat turning the pages without really looking at them. Ramona could tell she was trying to think what to say when she faced her father.

When Mr. Quimby came home from work, he left an armload of groceries in the kitchen before he came into the living room. "Hi, kids," he said, and when he looked at Beezus said, "Well, well, what have we here?"

Beezus dropped the magazine to face her father, ready to defend her ears. "They are my ears and I used my own money," she informed him. "I don't care what you say."

"Relax, Beezus." Mr. Quimby kissed the top of her head and said, "So our little girl is growing up. I'm surprised you didn't have your nose pierced while you were at it." He rumpled her hair affectionately.

"Dad, don't be silly," said Beezus, obviously relieved. "You know I wouldn't do a thing like that."

"You never can tell," said Mr. Quimby. "Kids today . . ." He left to change out of his supermarket clothes.

Beezus fell back in her chair and said, "Whew. That's over."

Ramona felt the same way. Now, if she ever wanted her ears pierced, which was hard to imagine, but if she ever should, all she would have to say was, Beezus had *her* ears pierced. And then when Roberta's turn came—Ramona did not even want to think of Roberta's tender little ears being shot with a thing that looked like a staple gun.

"Ramona, time to set the table," Mrs. Quimby called out.

"Okay," said Ramona, but she was thinking about Beezus growing up and about what it would be like to grow up herself. She felt the way she felt when she was reading a good book. She wanted to know what would happen next.

✦ 5 ✦
The Princess
and the Witch

Ramona was impatient to go to Daisy's house again, especially now that Beezus was talking so much about the upcoming party. She liked the Kidds' big untidy house with a dog, a cat, and a big brother. She also liked licking juice bars while watching *Big Hospital*. When the next visit was arranged, Ramona and Daisy ran from the school bus to Daisy's house. Jeremy was already lounging in front of the television set watching an ice hockey game.

The girls exchanged looks. "Germy, aren't you going to walk Mutley?" Daisy asked as if the dog were all she had on her mind. On hearing his name, Mutley raised his head, decided Daisy's words were not important, and rested his nose on his paws once more.

"Nope." Jeremy was definite. "And no, I'm not going to let you have the TV this time."

"Oh, well." Daisy was used to her big brother. "Come on, Ramona, let's go upstairs to my room and play dress-up."

"Nice try," said Jeremy.

As the girls climbed the stairs, Ramona could not help thinking that if the Quimbys' house had a second story they would have more bedrooms, and she and Beezus would not always be arguing over whose turn it was to dust the crowded space they now had to share because Roberta had Ramona's old room. Daisy, Ramona could see, was not neat at all.

Daisy pulled a carton to the center of her room and began to pull out clothes: satins, velvets, hats

71

with flowers and veils, a long black cape, high-heeled shoes.

"Wow!" breathed Ramona. "Where did you get all this?"

"Oh—around," said Daisy. "Mom collected most of it for me, because she loved to dress up when she was my age, only she couldn't find much to dress up in."

Nice mom, thought Ramona as she chose a long red dress with a flounce around the bottom and slipped it over her head.

Daisy pulled out a long yellow dress trimmed with little things that glittered, but before she poked her head into it she pulled off her slacks. "Dresses don't look good over pants, and besides, I like the swishy feeling against my legs," she explained.

Ramona, deciding she was right, pulled her pants off, too. Her dress felt smooth and silky against her bare legs. She snatched up a hat trimmed with some battered roses and set it on her head. Then she pulled off her shoes (her nice

shoes!) and stuck her feet into high-heeled sandals, which made her glamorous, she felt, even if they were too big. "Look! I'm a star!" Ramona lifted her arms as if she were a dancer before she clonked across the room to look at herself in the mirror. "I'm gorgeous," she announced, pretending she had long blond hair. "I'm beautiful. I'm me, gorgeous, beautiful me!"

"I'm Miss America." Daisy twirled around. "I'm so beautiful all the other girls in the competition went home."

Both girls clonked around, turning and swishing as if they were in a television fashion show. When they both turned their ankles and fell off their shoes, they collapsed on the bed in a fit of giggles.

Then Ramona discovered a long pink dress and because she was already gorgeous and beautiful decided to promote herself to princess. She quickly changed while Daisy switched from Miss America to a witch in a long black velvet gown and a small green hat with only three small holes in the veil. "I'm wicked!" cried Daisy.

"Great," said Ramona. "I never liked books with nice witches."

"I'm going to shut the beautiful princess in a dungeon!" Daisy made a witch face.

"Where are you going to find a dungeon to shut me in?" Ramona was a defiant princess.

"That's easy." The wicked witch pushed aside the clothes in her closet to reveal a small door, which she opened. Behind it was a dark space under the eaves, which was the attic.

Inside, in the half-light, Ramona saw a few boards laid across the joists to make a place for storing luggage. Beyond, Ramona could see, barely, the lath and plaster that made the ceilings of the rooms downstairs.

"See!" cried Daisy. "The wicked witch is going to shut the beautiful princess in the dark dungeon full of rats and feed her bread and water." She grabbed Ramona and pushed her toward the closet within a closet.

"No, she isn't!" cried Ramona, twisting away from Daisy. "The princess is going to throw the witch in the dungeon and feed her cold oatmeal!"

"Yuck," gagged Daisy. She shoved Ramona. Ramona shoved back. One shoe fell off. Daisy pushed harder and shoved Ramona through the little door into the dim space beyond. Ramona, in one shoe, stepped on her pink dress, lost her balance, turned, grabbed at nothing, and stepped off the boards onto the lath and plaster. There was an ominous cracking sound beneath her feet.

"Oh, no!" cried Daisy.

"Help!" shouted Ramona as the lath began to break beneath her weight, and she found herself sinking. Daisy screamed. The lath made snapping sounds. The pink dress ripped. Ramona heard bits of plaster hitting something below and felt her legs being scratched as the pink dress bunched up around her waist. Her other shoe fell off and hit something downstairs with a thump. She heard Mrs. Kidd cry out, "Oh my!"

Jeremy yelled, "Hey!" Mutley barked.

Desperate, Ramona bent forward over the joist to stop her fall and searched frantically with her feet to find something to stand on. There was noth-

ing, only air. Above her, rain pattered on the roof.

"Ramona, hang on!" Daisy called out. "Jeremy, come quick!"

"I'm hanging." Ramona was terrified. The sharp edge of the joist was pressing into her waist and her legs were cold. She wondered how much longer she could hang on. What if there really were rats in the attic? Dust was everywhere. Ramona sneezed. Below, Mutley barked harder, as if he were warning off an intruder. "Hurry," she wailed. On the television a referee blew a whistle and a crowd roared.

"They're coming," cried equally terrified Daisy, grabbing at the back of the pink dress. Thumping feet were heard on the stairs.

In a moment Jeremy pushed his sister aside and, standing on the boards, seized Ramona under the arms and tugged. "Dumb kids" was his comment.

"Ow," said Ramona. Jeremy tugged harder and managed to pull her out of the hole she had made. "Yow!" escaped from Ramona even though she was grateful to be rescued. As she was pulled out of the hole, she had a glimpse below of the dining room table covered with rubble.

"Oh, you poor child." Mrs. Kidd was filled with sympathy, concern, and relief.

Ramona was so glad to be standing on the hard floor with the remains of the pink dress heaped around her feet that she began to cry.

Mrs. Kidd hugged her and murmured, "There, there. You're safe now. Everything is all right."

"No, it isn't," wept Ramona. "I made a big hole in the floor—ceiling—"

"Whatever," said Jeremy, and left the room to clump down to the television set.

"Thank you," sniffled Ramona, remembering her manners even though Jeremy had left. "You saved my life." She began to cry harder. She had broken the ceiling and could never come to the Kidds' house again and she and Daisy couldn't be best friends and she would be left with Howie and messy old Willa Jean to play with and—

"Daisy, find Ramona some Kleenex," said Mrs. Kidd. Daisy produced a box from her dresser.

Ramona mopped her nose and eyes as Mrs. Kidd helped her down the stairs.

"I'll get her pants," said Daisy.

Downstairs, in the bathroom, Mrs. Kidd pulled off the pink dress. "Oh, my dear—" she said when she saw Ramona's legs. She began to clean the scratches with cotton and stinging liquid from a bottle. Then she covered them with Band-Aids, all sizes. When she had finished, Ramona gave a final sniff. Mrs. Kidd washed her face, kissed her, and said, "There. You're as good as new."

A fresh worry, paying for the damage, crept into Ramona's mind. Payday, the checks her mother wrote to pay bills, taxes, and all those grown-up things whirled around in her mind.

"That was some hole you made," said Jeremy as she and Mrs. Kidd went into the living room, where Clawed was peeking out from under the couch. Mutley, his tail drooping, looked anxious.

Ramona suddenly had a new thought. If Daisy hadn't been trying to shut her in a dungeon, none of this would have happened. Maybe it was Daisy's fault. Maybe she should be angry with Daisy. She was confused. She didn't want to be angry with her best friend. Still . . . she didn't know what to think.

Only then did Ramona gather her courage to look toward the dining room, where she saw in the ceiling a dark hole edged with broken lath and bits of plaster. The dining room table was covered with dust, rubble, and, in the midst of the mess, one high-heeled sandal. And the table had been set for—this made Ramona feel really bad—five places, one for her. Suddenly she didn't want to stay for dinner. She wanted to go home. She wanted to be home with her own mother comforting

her for her scratches and for the loss of her best friend. She looked at Daisy, wanting to say, It was all your fault for pushing me, but she did not say it, not in front of Mrs. Kidd. She would wait until school Monday and then she would—

Mrs. Kidd put her arm around Ramona. "Would you rather not stay for dinner?" she asked. Ramona nodded. "Then come along," said Mrs. Kidd. "I'll have you home in a jiffy."

"Ramona—" Daisy was blinking back tears. "It was all my fault. I—I shouldn't have pushed."

Ramona instantly felt both ashamed and much better. So often things that went wrong turned out to be her mistake. She should have known Daisy wasn't the kind of girl to blame people. "No, it wasn't your fault. It was both our faults, I guess." Ramona hesitated. "Promise you won't tell the kids at school."

Daisy crossed her heart, smiled shakily, and said, "Of course, if the beautiful princess had gone peacefully to the dungeon—"

Ramona interrupted, "And if the witch had been a nice witch—"

Daisy finished for her. "The kind you don't like to read about."

Ramona managed to smile back over her shoulder as she followed Mrs. Kidd out the door. On the way home she ventured a question that had been hovering in the back of her mind. "Will—will it cost a lot of money to fix the ceiling?" she asked Mrs. Kidd.

Mrs. Kidd patted Ramona's knee. "Don't worry about it. It was an accident, and I'm sure our insurance will take care of it. And you know something? Even before we moved in, I didn't like the color of the dining room. Now we have an excuse to repaint it."

Ramona felt so much better, except for the scratches and stiffness in her legs, that she began to consider the drama of the afternoon.

When Mrs. Kidd delivered her to the Quimbys' door, she merely said to Mrs. Quimby, "Ramona had a little accident. She will tell you about it."

It was a big accident, thought Ramona, pleased that Mrs. Kidd did not spoil her chance to tell. She really was a nice mother, the nicest she had ever known, next to her own, of course.

Mrs. Quimby immediately wanted to know what had happened but was distracted by Roberta. Ramona stalled for time by going to the bathroom and by darting into her room. When she came out, the family was seated at the dinner table. She then had the attention of her entire family, even Roberta, who was lying in her playpen nearby. Mrs. Quimby said, "Ramona, I thought you were going to have dinner at Daisy's house. And what did her mother mean about a little accident?"

Ramona assumed a sorrowful expression. "I was going to stay, but a terrible thing happened." Her family stopped eating. Ramona paused dramatically. Here was her chance to keep Beezus from talking so much about Abby and the party.

"Yes. Go on," said Mr. Quimby.

Ramona took a deep breath. "I broke the ceiling"—another dramatic pause—"I broke it all to smithereens and it's going to cost a bazillion dollars to fix and it fell all over the dining room and made a terrible mess, so I decided not to stay for dinner."

Mr. Quimby became more impatient. "Ramona, get to the point. What on earth are you talking about?"

Ramona basked in the attention. "I was a princess trying to escape from a wicked witch who was shutting me in a dungeon, and there I was all alone in the dark with spiders and bats—well, maybe not bats"—Ramona felt if she exaggerated too much her family would not believe her—"and I was terrified because the wicked witch was about to break down the door"—maybe she was stretching the truth a tiny bit, but perhaps no one would notice—"and I was terrified because I felt something bump against my leg, something big, something evil and crawly"—of course, suitcases weren't evil and crawly, but by then Ramona did not want to spoil her story with the truth—"and I was so terrified all alone in the creepy dark full of cobwebs that I tried to flee—"

"Eeee!" crowed Roberta.

"Ramona." Mrs. Quimby spoke quietly. "I think you're getting carried away."

Beezus, who had been quiet until now, spoke up. "So you stepped back on the unfinished part of the attic and fell through the ceiling. I know all about those attics because mothers were always telling us to stay off the lath and plaster, and I know someone who really did fall through."

Of course, Ramona was annoyed with Beezus for spoiling her story. "Sort of like that," she admitted with a scowl.

Mrs. Quimby was shocked. "Why, Ramona— Did you fall all the way through? You might have been seriously hurt."

"I hung on, but I was wounded." Ramona tried to regain her family's sympathy. "My legs got all scratched and scraped and it hurt a lot. I was in agony." There, take that, Beezus, she thought. "And then a handsome prince, I mean Daisy's brother, rescued me."

"Jeremy Kidd?" Beezus began to laugh. "He's in my math class. Wait till I tell him you called him a handsome prince!"

"Don't you dare!" Ramona was furious.

"Girls!" warned Mr. Quimby. "Beezus, there are some things we keep in the family."

Beezus stopped laughing. Finally she asked, "Weren't you wearing pants?"

Ramona said in her most dignified way, "Princesses don't wear pants." She paused and added, "Unless they are in disguise."

The family found this funny. Beezus recovered enough to say, "You must have looked weird, just your bare legs hanging down from the ceiling."

And my underpants, thought Ramona in horror, not having pictured the scene from below until this moment. Did I fall far enough for them to show? What if Jeremy saw them? She could never face him again. She could see that her family was hiding their smiles at the picture of Ramona's bare legs hanging from the ceiling. This made Ramona sulky. "It really did hurt, because I was wounded. I bled." That ought to impress her family.

Her father patted her hand. "I know it was painful and you could have been badly hurt."

"But I was brave." Ramona held her head high.

"I hung on with all my might and main." She wasn't quite sure what that meant. She had read it in a book someplace and it sounded right.

"Maybe you have a fairy godmother," suggested Mrs. Quimby.

A best friend is better, thought Ramona.

"Maybe," agreed Mr. Quimby, "but I think she has been reading fairy tales."

"I like fairy tales," said Ramona. "Fairy tales always have happy endings." She paused before she added, "And so does mine, I guess." Her family had paid attention to her and she still had a best friend. Then she thought to herself, A happy ending except for my underpants showing.

✦ 6 ✦
The Party

Before Ramona's scratches healed and her Band-Aids were pulled off, Ramona had grown bored with her sister's party invitation, the shopping, and most of all with the telephone calls. Beezus seemed always to be talking on the telephone. Boredom did not prevent Ramona from listening to her sister's half of the conversations: "I'm sorry. I won't be able to baby-sit that evening. I'm going to a party." "If George won't come, maybe you could ask Randy. He's only a semi-creep." "I just love my new skirt. We found it on sale. Have you bought yours yet?"

Then there were dancing lessons given by Mr. Quimby with much twirling and *step, slide, step, step, slide, step*. One evening when the lesson was finished and Beezus went off to do her homework, Mr. Quimby held out his hand to Ramona. "Let's give it a try," he said. Ramona shook her head. It all looked so silly.

Silliness did not stop Ramona from telling Daisy about the dancing lesson or from giving her a demonstration when she came to the Quimbys' after school. The girls stepped and slid, getting in the way of each other's feet, until, laughing, they fell over on the couch.

Another evening when Beezus was talking on the telephone, Ramona heard her father say to her mother, "I'll be glad when this party is over and we can all settle down again."

Mrs. Quimby lowered her voice, which of course made Ramona listen harder. "I'm glad Beezus is finally coming out of her shell. She has always been such a quiet girl. I do hope she has a good time. It could be a terrible letdown."

This conversation was a surprise to Ramona. She had assumed Beezus would have a good time twirling and gliding and eating good things. Maybe not. Maybe their mother was right.

Mrs. Quimby was not the only one concerned. When the girls were in bed, Beezus confided, "I hope Daddy's dancing isn't too old-fashioned."

"Daddy's a good dancer," said Ramona, loyal to their father even though his dancing did not look like some of the dancing she had seen on television.

Finally, to the relief of everyone, the day of the party arrived. Beezus washed her hair in the afternoon and was so nervous and excited she could scarcely eat her dinner. Afterward she lingered in the bath. "Whew!" said Ramona as perfume from bubble bath wafted down the hall.

At last Beezus appeared, ready for the party. "Ta-dah!" she announced as she came into the living room. "Do I really look all right?" She was

wearing her new long skirt, a pretty blouse, small gold hoops in her ears, and her hiking shoes that laced above her ankles. Her hair was shining, her cheeks pink.

"You look lovely, dear," said Mrs. Quimby, "but—ah—don't you think you should change your shoes?"

"Oh, Mom, nobody wears party shoes anymore these days." She gave her mother a pitying look.

"Oh," said her mother. "I didn't know."

"I think you look great." Ramona was impressed by the change in Beezus but somehow missed her plain big sister. Oh, well, at least her feet still looked sensible. Will I look like that someday? she wondered as she put her hand to her own hair and decided maybe she should brush it more often, the way her mother was always telling her.

Mrs. Quimby kissed Beezus and said, "Have a good time, dear. But don't you think you should wear a coat? This is November, you know."

"Oh, Mo-*ther*," said Beezus. "I don't want to wrinkle my new blouse. Besides, it's not like it's snowing or anything."

"I'll turn on the car heater," reassured Mr. Quimby. "We can't wrinkle that blouse."

Ramona suddenly did not want to let go of her sister. "Can I come, too?" she asked.

"Sure. Come along," Mr. Quimby said. The ride was made in silence with Beezus sitting up straight in the backseat and unwrinkled. In spite of the car heater she hugged her arms to keep warm. When they pulled up in front of Abby's house, Beezus said in anguish, "Dad, what do I do? My hands are all clammy."

"Don't worry, you'll do fine," said her father, "and it will all be over by eleven o'clock." After he dropped Beezus off among the arriving guests, he said, almost as if he were speaking to himself, "Well, there goes our little girl."

Ramona moved as close to her father as her seat belt would permit. "You still have me," she reminded him.

"That's right." Her father patted her knee. "And Roberta."

"Yes," whispered Ramona with a tiny sigh. She

loved her baby sister, but sometimes she wished her father did not have quite so many daughters.

When the two returned home, Mrs. Quimby looked up from her book (she did not have many pages left) and said, as if her thoughts were far away, "I'll never forget my first dance. It was in the school gym, and the only boy who asked me to dance I didn't want to dance with. He was a weird little fellow who grew up to be an interesting man, but at the time I wanted to dance with a tall, handsome boy. Silly me. I was a real wallflower and spent most of the evening hiding in the girls' bathroom with a couple of other miserable wallflowers."

Ramona was indignant. Stupid boys, not asking her nice mother to dance. She hoped Beezus wasn't hiding in the bathroom, even though the Alexanders' bathroom was sure to be nicer than a school bathroom. Their bathroom wouldn't have scratchy tan paper towels.

When her father told her to stop stalling and go to bed, Ramona lay awake thinking. She would never hide in a bathroom. She would march right up and ask a boy to dance if she ever wanted to do such a silly thing as dance.

Even though Ramona thought that dancing was silly, she wanted her sister to have a good time. She even said a little prayer as she lay awake, waiting, full of hope and curiosity. The minute she heard her father drive off to bring Beezus home, Ramona bounced out of bed and went into the living room, where her mother was finally finishing *Moby Dick*. Of course Mrs. Quimby said, "Ramona, you should be in bed asleep." Parents always said that.

Ramona ignored this remark and snuggled up under her mother's arm. She loved moments alone with her mother, which made her feel cozy and protected. She must have nodded off, for suddenly there was Beezus, her eyes still shining, her cheeks still pink. The rest of her face was unrecognizable. She was wearing dark red lipstick and green eye-shadow.

"Wow!" was Ramona's comment. "What happened to you?"

Beezus dropped into a chair and laughed.

Mrs. Quimby laughed as well, distracted from Beezus's new makeup by her relief at seeing her happy.

Ramona spoke up before Beezus could answer. "What's so funny?" she asked.

"Boys," said Beezus. "Boys are funny."

"Who says boys are funny?" Mr. Quimby had come in from the garage. "I was a boy once. I wasn't funny."

"I say boys are funny," said Beezus. "So do all the girls."

Mrs. Quimby asked, "What do boys do that is so funny?"

Beezus explained. "Except for one boy, they wouldn't even come in the house. One boy brought a miniature chess set and he and another boy played chess under the porch light. The others just sort of flopped around or tried standing on their hands in the wet grass. Some boys who weren't even invited joined in. There was a lot of whooping and yelling and neighbors coming out to see what was going on. One boy pulled a night crawler out of the lawn and chased another boy around with it. You know the stuff boys do. Mrs. Alexander got all upset because she wants Abby to be popular, and she wasn't being popular with all the boys sitting outside acting like a bunch of little kids. Somebody must have called the police, because we saw them drive by, but they kept on going."

"What about the boy in the house?" asked Mr. Quimby.

"He watched TV," Beezus explained. "Nobody paid any attention to him. The other boys said they had just come for the food."

Sounds like Yard Ape, Ramona thought, and Howie might bring a chess set.

"Poor hungry boys," said Mr. Quimby. "I hope somebody fed them."

"Oh, sure," said Beezus as if this was not important. "The girls had fun experimenting with free samples of lipstick and all the other free samples Mrs. Alexander gets when she buys cosmetics."

"I wondered what happened to your face," said Mrs. Quimby with a smile, "but I was afraid to ask."

"Mrs. Alexander wears lots of makeup," Beezus continued, "and her hair is a funny color. She wears it all fluffed up and it looks something like those coppery things we scour pans with."

"You look weird, like a vampire or something" was Ramona's comment. "What about the dancing?"

"That's the best part. We didn't have to dance," said Beezus. "Some girls were disappointed, but we sort of played Monopoly and Scrabble. Mostly we talked about—oh, you know—and had a good time anyway, and then the boys began to yell that they were hungry. Mrs. Alexander just about had a fit after paying for Abby's dancing lessons and everything, but we took sandwiches and punch and cookies out to them. Mrs. Alexander had old-fashioned food instead of pizza and stuff. They quieted down after that."

"What a relief," said Mr. Quimby. "I was worried about those poor hungry kids out there in the cold."

"Dad, you're just being silly." Beezus giggled

100

and continued, "I didn't really want to dance any-way. At least not yet, not until boys get over being such little kids."

"Well, how do you like that?" said Mr. Quimby. "My dancing lessons wasted. Those boys had prob-ably shined their shoes and didn't want girls step-ping all over them."

Ramona could see her sister was so happy she didn't mind being teased. "But what about the night crawler?" she asked.

"When we brought out the food, they threw it back in the grass," Beezus explained.

Ramona was only slightly disappointed. "Did you get anything to eat?" What was the point of a party without food?

"Of course," said Beezus. "You don't think we'd let the boys have everything, do you? We ate the salad and the ice cream."

"I'm so glad you had a good time, dear," said Mrs. Quimby. "Now wash your face *good* with soap and run along to bed. It's almost midnight."

Beezus paused in the doorway. "You know

something?" she asked. "I don't think Abby and I are the popular type. And you know something else? I don't care."

"I'm glad you feel that way," said Mrs. Quimby with a tender smile. "I wish I had been that sensible when I was your age."

"*C'est la vie*," said Beezus and, as she headed to the bedroom, added to Ramona, "That's French for 'That's life.'"

Ramona made a face. "*Au revoir.*" She had picked up a word or two of French herself.

"You, too, kiddo," said Mrs. Quimby to Ramona.

Ramona snuggled against her mother, stalling for time, and said, "I'm glad I have a nice plain mother instead of a mother with hair you could scour pans with." If she could postpone going to bed, she might get to hear what her parents would say about Beezus.

"Thank you." Mrs. Quimby smiled affectionately and rumpled Ramona's hair. "But compliments won't keep you out of bed. Now run along."

Ramona pattered on light feet down the hall and climbed into bed. Her next-to-last thought, before she fell asleep, was, I can't wait to tell Daisy. Her last thought was, I'm glad Beezus is still sensible on the inside.

⋆ 7 ⋆
The Grown-up Letter

It was almost Thanksgiving when Ramona decided that she liked Mrs. Meacham most of the time. Not that Mrs. Meacham did not have flaws. She did, in Ramona's opinion. Mrs. Meacham was enthusiastic about spelling and especially enjoyed words with silent letters such as *knit* and *wrist*. She was also a stickler for pronunciation and corrected anyone who said "gonna" or "shoulda." "If you don't pronounce correctly, you can't spell," she said much too often, Ramona thought.

Most of the fourth grade thought Mrs. Meacham had another flaw. She confiscated any notes written by her class that were sailed, passed, or dropped on desks. She then read them for misspelled words and, if she found one, added it to the list on the chalkboard: Words We Need to Work On. She then tore up the notes and threw the pieces in the wastebasket.

The fourth grade thought this was unfair, but Ramona was not much concerned. By the fourth grade she had learned to put up with teachers. She was not concerned, that is, until one day when Yard Ape, on his way to the pencil sharpener, dropped a

note on her desk. She picked it up and was about to read it when Mrs. Meacham said, "Ramona, bring the note to me." Trapped, Ramona obeyed.

Mrs. Meacham read it, smiled, and turned to the chalkboard, where she added one word to the list of Words We Need to Work On. That word was "Ramona." She then tore up the note and gave a little talk about not confusing *n* with *m*. Ramona, along with the rest of the class, then knew Yard Ape had written "Ranoma" instead of "Ramona." She glanced at him. He was looking straight ahead and even his ears were red. She had never seen Yard Ape embarrassed before. What could he have written in the note?

At recess all the boys chanted, "Danny loves Ramona! Danny loves Ramona!"

Daisy asked, "Didn't you get to read any of it?" Ramona shook her head, more curious than ever. She decided to ask Yard Ape, but he was so busy kicking a ball that he acted as if he had never met her. Oh, well. Now her class would have to study her name in spelling. Ramona liked that.

Yard Ape continued to avoid Ramona. When he wasn't paying attention in class, he was busy drawing a wristwatch in ink on his arm. On the bus he sat with the rowdy boys in the last seats.

As the winter rains beat against the classroom windows, Ramona plodded along with spelling, day after day, spelling most words right if she had worked hard, something she did not often do. On tests, if she spelled them all right, Mrs. Meacham wrote, "Keep up the good work!" on her paper. Ramona sometimes wondered if spelling correctly was worthwhile, because those who spelled all their words right were given what Mrs. Meacham called Reward Words to work on. These were really hard words, some with three syllables. Ramona did not feel rewarded.

At home Ramona's parents and sometimes Beezus sat beside her on the couch and went over spelling words with Ramona, who squirmed, unfastened and refastened the Velcro on her shoes, or tried to put one foot behind her head. Her parents sighed. Beezus said, "Oh, grow up, Ramona."

"I am a potential grown-up," Ramona said with dignity, pleased to have used a Reward Word. She looked at Roberta lying in her playpen with her chewed-up bear and felt a moment of pity for her baby sister and what lay ahead of her in growing up, especially spelling.

All this made Ramona feel surrounded by words. There were words everyplace she looked: in books and newspapers, on signs and television, on cereal boxes and milk cartons. The world, Ramona decided, was full of people who used their dictionary skills and probably weren't any fun.

Then one day when Ramona was riding on the school bus going to Daisy's house, she glanced out the window and happened to notice a license plate on a car in the next lane. Instead of numbers it had letters: LIBARY. "Daisy, look!" she said. "They left out a letter." Ramona was sure of the spelling of *library* because she went to the branch library once a week and saw the word above the door every time she entered.

"You'd better tell Mrs. Meacham," said Daisy.

The next morning Ramona approached Mrs. Meacham, planted herself squarely in front of her teacher, and said, "I saw a license plate with *library* spelled with only one *r*, and that is wrong."

"Good for you, Ramona," said Mrs. Meacham. "I know that license plate. It belongs to the county librarian."

Ramona was indignant. "If she can't spell, why is she a librarian? Librarians should know how to spell."

Mrs. Meacham laughed and said, "I'm glad you think so, Ramona, but the state of Oregon allows

only six letters on personalized license plates. I am sure the librarian is really an excellent speller."

"Oh," said Ramona, disappointed. She wanted a grown-up to be wrong for a change. She was tired of the rightness of grown-ups.

That same day, late in the afternoon, when Ramona was grouchy because her mother had turned off *Big Hospital,* she was reading when she came across a strange word: *asinine.* She did not want to spoil the pleasure of reading by looking it up, so she called out to anyone listening, "What does *as-i-nine* mean?"

Beezus answered, "Stupid, dumb, silly, acting like a mule." She was cross because she was having trouble with French verbs.

Ramona scowled, annoyed by her sister's superiority. "I didn't ask to have my vocabulary built. I just wanted to know what it meant."

"Like I said. Stupid, dumb, foolish, mulish," said Beezus. "Like you."

That was too much for Ramona. She threw down her book and called out, "Mother, Beezus called me a bad name."

"Well, you are," said Beezus. "You are stupid, dumb, foolish, mulish, and asinine. Everybody has to learn how to spell."

"I wasn't asking about spelling, and just because you're in high school, you think you're so big!" countered Ramona. "Well, I think you're mean."

"At least I keep my half of our room neat," said Beezus.

Mrs. Quimby came into the room. "Girls! Stop it this minute. I've had enough of this nonsense. Ramona, you are being foolish, yes, asinine about learning to spell, and Beezus, you are being stupid when you call your sister names. This sort of thing will only escalate into more name-calling. This is no example to set for Roberta."

The girls were startled. Their mother rarely spoke so sharply. They looked at each other with looks that said, Stupid? Foolish? Us?

"And furthermore," said Mrs. Quimby, "I don't want to hear any more bickering about whose turn it is to clean up your room." With that she stalked out of the room to look after fussing Roberta, who was feverish. The pediatrician had given her a shot to prevent her from getting whooping cough.

"We're nice most of the time." Beezus regretted name-calling. "We wouldn't be normal if we didn't forget sometimes."

"I don't suppose Roberta will be one of those people who grows up just naturally knowing how to spell." Ramona sighed, defeated. "Not with me for a role model."

"Spelling is just one of those things you have to *do*," said Beezus, "and there's always the dictionary."

"Boring," said Ramona, and thought fondly of Daisy, herself a good speller, who never criticized Ramona's spelling, because she could tell what she meant.

After that, Ramona and Beezus stopped bickering so much, and Ramona continued, with tiresome help from her family, to muddle along with spelling. When progress report time came, she delivered her envelope to her mother without peeking. Mrs. Quimby read the report, smiled, kissed Ramona, and said, "Good work. I'm proud of you." Then she turned the report over to the Habits and Attitudes section, frowned, and read aloud, "Ramona's spelling will improve when she decides she wants it to improve." Mrs. Quimby looked at Ramona, but all she said was "Well?"

"Mrs. Meacham is *mean*," Ramona explained. "If we get all the spelling words right, she gives us hard words and calls them Reward Words as if they were some kind of treat. They aren't. They are really, really hard words like *foreign* and *quarantine*, the kind of words where you don't know which letter comes first. I think you should go talk to Mrs. Meacham and tell her she's mean."

"And what do you think she would say to that?" Mrs. Quimby asked.

Ramona thought a moment. "She'd say I am a horrible, stupid child with bad habits and attitudes, the worst fourth grader she's ever had, and she can't wait to get rid of me and she never wants to see me again as long as she lives."

Mrs. Quimby did not seem upset. "Do you

really think Mrs. Meacham would say that?"

Once more Ramona thought before she answered in a small voice, "No, but I'm tired of spelling."

Mrs. Quimby said, "So am I. So is your whole family."

"Except Roberta," Ramona reminded her mother.

Mrs. Quimby ignored the interruption. "From now on, you're on your own." She meant it, because after that no one said, "Come on, Ramona, let's go over your spelling words." Nobody said, "How about a little spelling before bedtime?" Nobody cared about Ramona's spelling.

Ramona began to feel that no one cared about her, either. Her mother was busy reading a new book for her book club or comforting drooly Roberta, who was teething, Beezus was either talking on the telephone or doing her homework, and Mr. Quimby was in the basement refinishing his grandmother's chest of drawers for Roberta's room.

That left Daisy, who had no trouble spelling.

One afternoon when she had come to Ramona's house, the girls were looking for something to do. Daisy picked up the sports section of the newspaper, which was lying on the coffee table, and began to read aloud as if she were an excited television announcer, "'Crash! Splash! $25 Cash Back! No down payments for six months!'"

Ramona picked up another part of the paper and read in a stern voice, "'Stop sneezing! Get rid of dust, mold, and fungus with our duct clean-

up system'"—here, a dramatic pause—"'and keep it clean!'"

Both girls found this funny.

"Sounds like what Jeremy's room needs," remarked Daisy before she read in a dreamy voice, "'Planning a romantic wedding?'"

"Not right away," said Ramona, scanning the newspaper. "Here's a funny letter somebody wrote to some people who do income tax stuff. They put it in their ad."

"Boring," said Daisy.

Ramona ignored her and read, "'You J. K. Barker people really know your stuff. I shoulda come here last year, and I'm gonna come here next year.'" She frowned her disapproval.

Daisy was indignant. "They shouldn't put words like *gonna* and *shoulda* in the newspaper. Mrs. Meacham wouldn't like it."

"Or maybe we should show it to Mrs. Meacham," suggested Ramona, "so she would know it is okay to use them because they are in the newspaper."

Daisy was doubtful. "You know Mrs. Meacham. She'll march right down to the newspaper with her red pencil and—"

"I know!" Ramona was inspired. "Let's write to the tax people. I bet they made up the letter themselves."

Daisy was enthusiastic. Ramona found paper and an envelope, and the girls went to work composing their letter. "Dear Tax People," Ramona wrote, because her cursive was better than Daisy's. "There are no such words as gonna and shoulda which you put in your ad. You set a bad example for children who are learning to spell. We think you made up the letter yourself." Ramona added the last sentence. "There are better words than stuff." Daisy read the letter carefully to make sure they had not misspelled words. They both signed it, including their ages. Ramona addressed the envelope and included the Quimbys' return address. Then they ran to the corner mailbox, mailed it, and forgot about it. They had other things to think about.

That was why Ramona was surprised a week later when she came home from school and her mother handed her a long envelope addressed to Miss Ramona Quimby. Nobody had ever called her "Miss" except when they were joking or were cross with her. This looked serious. The return address read, "J. K. Barker. Certified Public Accountant."

"Ramona, are you having problems with your income tax?" Mrs. Quimby asked, behaving as if she were serious even though she was joking.

"Oh, Mother. You know my allowance isn't that big." Ramona tore open the envelope and pulled out a crisp sheet of paper, a real grown-up business letter addressed to her and to Daisy. Only then did Ramona remember the letter they had written, a letter they did not expect to be answered. This letter read: "Dear Ramona and Daisy: I goofed and you caught me! I did make up the letter in the newspaper, and I promise never to do it again, not when two sharp-eyed nine-year-olds read my advertisements. You must do good work in school and are sure to do well in life. When you earn millions of dollars, please bring your income tax work to my office. Cordially, J. K. Barker."

Ramona was so impressed she reread the letter. Grown-ups almost never admitted they goofed.

"May I see?" asked Mrs. Quimby. When she had read the letter, she said, "This is great. Mrs. Meacham should be proud of you."

Ramona ran to the telephone. Daisy, as she had expected, was every bit as excited as she was. Like Ramona, she could not wait to show Mrs. Meacham their real grown-up letter.

The next morning Daisy met Ramona as she got off the school bus. Together they accosted Mrs. Meacham and held out J. K. Barker's letter. Mrs. Meacham read it and said, "Good for you! This world needs more people like you to keep things in order. May I read this to the class?" Of course the girls agreed, and while she read it they tried to look modest. Then their teacher fastened it with thumbtacks to the bulletin board for all to behold.

Everyone was impressed, even Susan. Yard

Ape, looking straight ahead, smiled, but Ramona noticed that out of the corner of his eye he was looking at her.

Ramona felt good, better than she had felt since the first day of fourth grade.

◆ 8 ◆
Peas

The rainy winter days passed quickly. Thanksgiving came and not long afterward Christmas vacation. Ramona missed Daisy, who went with her family to visit her grandparents. When she returned, the girls spent an afternoon dressing up Roberta in the clothes she had received for Christmas. Roberta was agreeable to having a dress pulled over her head, her arms stuffed into a sweater, her head shoved into caps. She enjoyed the girls' admiration. She was not so happy about a pair of crocheted slippers with ears and tails that looked like rabbits, a gift from Howie's grandmother, who enjoyed crocheting. Roberta did not care for the slippers. She puckered up, ready to cry.

"Come on, Roberta," coaxed Ramona. "You'll have bunnies for feet. See."

Bunny feet did not interest Roberta, especially when she was beginning to feel tired. She began to fuss.

"Maybe the bunnies tickle her feet," suggested Daisy.

"Roberta, feel how nice and soft the bunny is." Ramona pulled a slipper over Roberta's curling toes. Roberta began to howl. She was not going to wear those slippers, and Ramona could not make her.

"Okay, okay," said Ramona, giving in. Roberta, she could see, was no longer the happy, cooing baby she had been except when teething or when the pediatrician had given her a shot to keep her from getting sick. She now had a will of her own. She's growing up, thought Ramona, like me.

Not long after this, when Ramona splashed home from the bus in the icy rain, her mother called out as she opened the back door, "Don't step on Roberta."

After the wind and rain, the kitchen felt warm and cozy. Mm-m. Ramona inhaled. Meat loaf for dinner. She would not have to struggle to cut it with a knife. Roberta was sitting in the middle of the floor pounding on a pan with a wooden spoon. Ramona sat down on the floor beside her to pull off her wet boots. "Mother, guess what?" she began.

Mrs. Quimby, too busy to guess what, did not answer. Instead she said, "Would you please give me a hand with Roberta? This is your father's bowling night, and I want to have dinner early. I'm behind because Roberta pushed a jar of tomato sauce onto the floor in the market." Moving quickly, she picked up Roberta, said "Upsy-daisy," set her in her high chair, scooped up the pan and wooden spoon, and tossed them into the sink. She placed a plastic dish of Roberta's dinner and a cup with a spout on the high-chair tray, and handed Ramona a spoon.

Ramona examined Roberta's dinner. "What's this green stuff?" she asked as she tied a bib around Roberta's neck. Roberta, in a happy mood, squealed and patted her hands on the tray.

"Peas," answered their mother, busy rolling wet lettuce in a towel. "I was in a hurry and I found an old jar of baby food. I know Roberta has outgrown strained peas, but I didn't want to waste them."

"Yuck," said Ramona. The peas were unappetizing, and Roberta looked so innocent and trusting. Oh well, Roberta was the one who had to eat them. Spooning food into the baby's rosy mouth or guiding her little hand clutching her spoon made Ramona feel grown-up and responsible, a big sister for a change.

The telephone rang in the hall. Mrs. Quimby answered. "Oh, hello, Sally," she said.

A book club lady, Ramona thought. That meant a long, boring conversation. Maybe if she hurried she could see part of *Big Hospital* before her mother finished her conversation and told her to turn it off. Curly-haired Doctor had fallen in love with Blond Nurse, who was secretly married. . . .

Ramona couldn't wait to see what happened next. She decided to hold the spoon herself to feed Roberta more quickly.

Mrs. Quimby was saying, "Let's read a shorter book this time. I thought I would never finish *Moby Dick*."

Ramona dipped up a spoonful of cottage cheese. "Open wide," she said to Roberta. "Down the little red lane." That was what her mother said when she fed Roberta. Ramona opened her own mouth, because she was Roberta's role model. Roberta obediently imitated her and accepted the cottage cheese. "Good girl," said Ramona. Roberta smiled a messy smile and pounded her heels against the high chair.

Mrs. Quimby was saying, "I really enjoy our book club. Now that I am no longer working—not that looking after my daughters isn't work—I enjoy exercising my brain."

Ramona was surprised and a little hurt that her mother found her daughters work. Roberta reached for the spoon. Ramona held on to it because Roberta would finish faster if she was fed. Ramona tried strained peas next. "Come on, Roberta. Down the hatch," she said, using her father's words.

The hatch remained closed. Ramona tried to poke the spoon between Roberta's lips. Roberta did not care to be poked. She began to look stubborn. Ramona was growing impatient to get to the television. If the husband of Blond Nurse found out about Curly-haired Doctor—

Roberta kept her lips tightly closed. "Look, Roberta. Watch your big sister." Ramona opened her mouth wide, and after thinking it over, Roberta did the same. Ramona popped the peas into her mouth. Roberta frowned but accepted another spoonful. Then she leaned out of her chair, opened her mouth, and let peas dribble out onto the linoleum.

"Roberta!" cried Ramona. When Roberta looked worried, she changed the tone of her voice and said, "Yum-yum. Nice peas full of vitamins and good things." She smiled as she held a generous spoonful to Roberta's lips and thought, Horrid, nasty peas, before she said, "Open wide." When Roberta did as she was told, Ramona spooned in the peas.

With her mouth full of peas, Roberta looked both surprised and disappointed, as if her sister had betrayed her. Then she blew hard, spraying mushy, squishy, smelly green peas all over Ramona.

"Roberta!" cried Ramona, dropping the spoon on the high-chair tray and wiping her face on her sleeve. Roberta picked up the spoon, beat it in her

food, and crowed. Then, filled with glee at what she had done, she threw the spoon on the floor. Why bother with it when she had hands? She patted her food and rubbed her hair.

"Mother!" cried Ramona. "Roberta's making a mess."

"Cope, dear. I'm busy," answered Mrs. Quimby from the hall. "Just do the best you can."

"E-e-e!" squealed Roberta as she threw her cup on the floor. Before Ramona could unfurl a banner of paper towels to wipe Roberta's face, her hair, her high chair, everything, Roberta tried to pick up her dish, which was held fast by the suction cup. She scowled, picked up a handful of food instead, and let it plop out of her hand onto the floor. This pleased her so much she squealed again.

"Roberta! Naughty girl!" cried Ramona, wiping peas off her own face. She never wanted to smell peas again. Roberta looked as if her feelings were hurt.

This time Mrs. Quimby said, "Sorry, Sally. I hear a damsel in distress." And ended her book club conversation. When she saw the mess in the kitchen, she sighed, reached for a sponge, and said, "Well, this really has been one of those days."

Ramona tried to scrub peas out of Roberta's hair with a paper towel. She no longer felt like a big sister. She felt like a cross sister, even if Roberta was just a baby. Roberta smiled a peas-and-cottage-cheese-smeared smile.

"Don't worry about it, Ramona," said Mrs. Quimby. She sounded tired. "Messes are a part of being a mother. A big part, now that I think about it. What was it you started to tell me before the telephone rang?"

Ramona hesitated. Somehow her news no longer seemed important. "Oh, nothing much," she said as Mr. Quimby and Beezus came dripping through the back door. "Only that a photographer is coming to take our school pictures tomorrow, and Mrs. Meacham says we are going to have a valentine box in our room."

"Good," said Mrs. Quimby. "Grandpa Day and Aunt Bea always like to have your picture."

"Remember to say cheese," said Mr. Quimby as he stepped over peas and cottage cheese.

"Photographers always tell you to say that," said Beezus, the experienced older sister. She pulled off her raincoat and dropped it on a chair before she picked up Roberta's cup from the floor.

Mr. Quimby did not bother to take off his raincoat. He dampened a towel and began to wipe Roberta's hands and face. "I see that Third Daughter has a mind of her own," he remarked.

"E-e-e," squealed Roberta, happy to have her family waiting on her. That was the advantage of being a baby sister.

Feeling somewhat dejected because she had not been able to feed Roberta neatly, Ramona went off to her room to see what she could find to wear for her class picture.

The next morning Ramona put on a red plaid jumper and a white blouse with a ruffle around the collar. The shoulders and armholes were a little tight, but she loved the twirly pleated skirt, even if it had once belonged to Beezus. Under the skirt she wore a pair of play shorts so no boy could see her underpants if she happened to bend over. She brushed the back of her hair, although it wouldn't show in the picture.

"Isn't your dress a little too—" began Mrs. Quimby as Ramona picked up her lunch bag. She must have changed her mind because she finished with "You look very nice today, dear."

"Don't choke in that blouse," said Beezus. "It looks awfully tight."

Ramona ignored her sister and walked off to the bus stop feeling neat, clean, and beautiful. The rain had stopped, and even though the day was cold, she left her raincoat unfastened because, like Beezus, she wanted to arrive unwrinkled. She walked instead of skipped so her hair would stay flat. She resisted stomping in puddles.

Mrs. Pitt, busy picking up advertising circulars from her porch, said, "My, don't you look nice this morning?" Ramona smiled modestly. This was the sort of grown-up question that did not demand an answer.

"What are you all dressed up for?" asked Howie, who was eating his sandwich in the middle of the sidewalk.

"My picture," said Ramona.

"Big deal," said Howie.

"Are you drethed up for a party?" asked a little girl Ramona could tell was in the second grade because she had lost her two front teeth.

When Ramona reached her classroom, Mrs. Meacham, whose hair was freshly curled, smiled and said, "You look very nice today, Ramona."

"I know," answered Ramona modestly. She felt a shoulder seam in her blouse split.

"You're all dressed up like you think you're somebody," said Susan.

"I am somebody," said Ramona with a toss of her head. She managed to stay neat until just before spelling time, when the school secretary opened the door and beckoned to Mrs. Meacham, who said, "All right, boys and girls. Picture time. Line up and walk *quietly* to the library, where we will all wait *quietly* for our turn. And remember to smile. At our school learning is fun. Let's show our parents by smiling."

Ramona was glad to escape working on *ôr, ôr,* and *yŏŏr* words for a little while.

In the library a screen had been set up. On it was a picture of nothing in particular—clouds maybe, or shadows. The photographer was a young man with a lock of hair sticking straight up from the back of his head. "Hi, kids," he said. "My name is Bill." He pointed to a box of paper combs. "Make yourselves pretty." Some children took combs; others smoothed their hair with their hands. Bill motioned to the first girl in line, who as usual was Susan. Being first was important to Susan. He positioned her in front of the camera and said, "Say cheese," just as Beezus had predicted.

Susan said cheese. The camera clicked.

"Next!" said Bill as Susan stepped aside. A boy took her place. "Say cheese," ordered Bill. This went on over and over until it was Yard Ape's turn. He stood up straight, grinned, and after saying cheese did not step aside. "How come you always tell us to say cheese?" he asked. "Don't you get tired of it?"

"As a matter of fact I do, now that you mention it," answered Bill. "Next!"

It was Ramona's turn to step in front of the screen for "cheese."

Bill surprised her. "Say peas," he said.

Instantly Ramona thought of Roberta's spitting gooshy, smelly peas in her face. Ee-yew. Without thinking she scowled, wrinkled her nose as if smelling something bad, and pulled down the corners of her mouth. The camera clicked, the class laughed, and Bill said, "Next!" Ramona hesitated. "Move along," ordered Bill. "I have a gazillion kids waiting." Ramona moved. She began to feel as if the neck of her blouse was choking her, so she unbuttoned the top button. She wondered what her family would say when they saw her picture.

Gradually, as the day went on and the class became engrossed in the study of pioneers crossing the plains in their covered wagons, Ramona began to feel that perhaps her picture was not as

bad as she thought it was. Maybe Bill had snapped her picture a millionth of a second before she made a face. Of course. That was what had happened. Of course it was. Ramona spent the rest of the day feeling cute and perky even if her clothes were too tight.

9
Ramona Sits

Ramona put her class picture out of her mind entirely. She had other things to think about. "I wish I would hurry up and be old enough to baby-sit," she confided to Beezus one cold, wet morning as she watched her sister put on a new T-shirt she had bought with money she had earned. "I've had a lot of practice with Roberta when Mother is busy. I know I could do it."

Beezus looked thoughtful. "Maybe . . ." She was not so sure. She looked at her sister, who was pulling on her socks as she lay on her bed with her feet in the air. "You're really more of a cheerleader type."

"I am?" Ramona sat up, startled at this insight into her character. "How come?"

"Oh, you know—" Beezus airily waved her hand. "You're always jumping around and waving things."

Ramona did not know what to say, so she said, "I don't care. I still want to baby-sit."

That was why, one afternoon shortly before semester break, Ramona came home from school and faced her mother with a question: "If I'm not old enough to baby-sit, am I old enough to cat-sit?"

Mrs. Quimby thought a moment before she asked, "Are you asking about cats in general or about one specific cat?"

"Daisy's brother's cat, Clawed," explained Ramona. "The family is going down to Roseburg to be with Daisy's grandparents during semester break. They take their dog in the car, but they have to take Clawed to the Kitty Corner and Clawed will be unhappy because he will be shut up in a cage and nobody will pet him."

"Oh," said Mrs. Quimby.

"Mo-*ther*." Ramona was impatient. "Clawed is a really *nice* cat. He doesn't claw furniture or anything. Daisy said when he stayed at the Kitty Corner at Christmas he came home all grouchy. Besides, Daisy's mother will pay me for cat-sitting."

"Oh?" Mrs. Quimby smiled. "It sounds to me as if you and Daisy have this all figured out."

Ramona pressed on. "If Beezus can baby-sit, I don't see why—"

"Ramona," Mrs. Quimby, no longer smiling, interrupted. "I really can't drive you to Daisy's house every day to feed a cat. With Roberta it would be too much."

Ramona was not a girl to give up easily. "We could bring Clawed here. We used to have a cat." She took a deep breath and prepared for major pleading. If necessary she would even whine. "Puleeze, pu-*leeze*. I'll take care of him and everything. You wouldn't have to do a thing. And I just know Roberta would love to pet him."

Mrs. Quimby sighed. "Well—as long as you agree to be entirely responsible for him. How long did you say they would be gone?"

"Just a week," said Ramona. "Just a teeny tiny short week."

Mrs. Quimby's smile returned. "There is no such thing as a short week. A week is seven days, no more, no less. All right. You may look after Clawed for a week if Daisy's family can bring him here. But remember, he is your responsibility and no one else's."

Delighted to have a chance to be responsible, Ramona ran to the telephone to tell Daisy the good news.

Several days later Mrs. Kidd, Daisy, and Jeremy delivered yowling, angry Clawed in his carrier along with his litter box, a bag of litter, a brush, canned and dried cat food, two dishes, and a square carpet-covered construction with two holes, one above the other, each big enough for Clawed to hide in. "Jeremy built Clawed's scratching post himself." Daisy was proud of her brother. "We call it Clawed's kitty condo."

Ramona had not thought of Clawed's equipment. She had expected an unencumbered cat.

Mrs. Kidd unfastened the latch on the carrier. "This will be much better for Clawed," she said. "He will settle down as soon as he has a chance to look around. We can't thank you enough."

"That's perfectly all right," said Mrs. Quimby. "Ramona is eager to take care of him."

Clawed sat down and began to use his rough tongue to smooth his rumpled fur and to wash away the taint of his cage.

Ramona eyed the litter box. She had pictured herself holding and petting Clawed while she looked at television or read a book.

At that point Beezus came into the room, looked at Clawed, and said, "Don't expect *me* to empty his litter box. I am not the one who is responsible." Then she noticed Jeremy, quickly changed the tone of her voice, and said, "Oh— hello, Jeremy."

"Hello, Beatrice." Jeremy turned red.

"Come on, kids. We have a zillion things to do."

Mrs. Kidd hugged Ramona and said, "I thank you, Clawed thanks you, we all thank you. Oh—and don't forget to brush him every day. That way he won't throw up so many hair balls."

"You're welcome," said Ramona with as much enthusiasm as she could muster. She disliked the smell of canned cat food, and she did not want to think about hair balls.

Jeremy bent over to stroke Clawed. "So long, you old rascal. I'll miss you." Clawed rubbed against Jeremy's legs, and the family departed with the carrier, leaving Ramona in charge of the cat.

"Nice kitty." Ramona tried to mean it. Clawed paused in licking his paw to look at her. Then he continued washing as if he did not care to associate with her.

"Ramona, take the litter box to the basement." Mrs. Quimby spoke in a brisk, no-nonsense voice. Ramona knew she had no choice but to do as she was told. When she returned, Beezus was holding Roberta and saying, "See the kitty? See the nice kitty?" Roberta's thoughts did not show. She had not made up her mind about Clawed, who ignored everything but his own paw and fur.

"You might put out some food and water for him so he will feel more at home," suggested Ramona's mother.

Ramona spread newspapers on the floor in the corner of the kitchen, set out Clawed's dishes, and with the electric can opener opened a can of Pusspuddy. *Pee-yew.*

One whiff and she tried not to breathe. Clawed, recognizing the sound of a can opener, came running to investigate. "There, Your Royal Highness." Ramona spoke crossly. Clawed chose to ignore her. She tried to make up for speaking so disagreeably by stroking him, but Clawed merely turned his head long enough to give her a look that said, You are not my friend. After eating, he explored the house before he curled up in a hole in his kitty condo and stared balefully out at the Quimbys' living room. Then he went to sleep.

Later that evening Mrs. Quimby said to Ramona, "Bedtime for your boarder. You'd better shut him in the basement."

Clawed had different ideas. "Here, kitty, kitty,"

coaxed Ramona. Clawed glared from the hole in the post.

"Come on, puss-puss," wheedled Beezus, trying to help. After all, she really liked cats. Clawed ignored her, his chin still resting on his paws.

Mrs. Quimby reached into the hole and stroked the cat's head. "Good kitty," she whispered. Clawed closed his eyes.

"I'll show you how to deal with an old tomcat." Mr. Quimby picked up the carpeted post, turned it on its side, and dumped Clawed onto the carpet. "Catch him!" he directed.

Ramona tackled Clawed and picked him up. Clawed went limp. "Nice kitty-cat," she said, trying to make up for the indignity of his being dumped. He was heavier than she expected.

Mr. Quimby scratched Clawed's ear. "Into the basement, old boy," he said.

Ramona lugged the cat to the basement door, set him down on the top step, and closed the door quickly. She thought better of this unkindness, opened the door a crack, and said, "Nighty-night, Clawed."

The cat was silent. He was silent, that is, until the family was in bed asleep. He then began to protest. He yowled at the basement door, he meowed pitifully, and yowled some more. Except for Roberta, who always slept soundly, the whole family was awake.

"Ramona," Mr. Quimby called out. "Do something about that cat."

"What am I supposed to do?" asked Ramona, only half-awake.

"Just cope," said her father. This annoyed Ramona. Now that she was in the fourth grade, her parents often told her to cope when she wanted help.

Without bothering with slippers, she stumbled sleepily down the hall, faintly illuminated by the tiny green light on the electric toothbrush in the bathroom. The kitchen linoleum felt cold to her feet as she opened the basement door. "Come on, you old cat," she said, and felt Clawed brush against her nightgown. "See if I care what you do."

What Clawed did was sleep on the living room couch. He had won. In the morning, when the

Quimbys were getting out of bed, he yawned, stretched, went to his water dish, decided he didn't care for it, strolled into the bathroom, and drank out of the toilet. "You old scoundrel," muttered Mr. Quimby through the sound of his electric razor.

Now that Clawed had made it clear to the family that he was going to set the rules for his treatment, he turned into a mostly agreeable cat, and as Ramona had predicted, Roberta was fascinated by a creature smaller than she was. She crawled after him, patted his fur, squealed with pleasure. Clawed did not seem to mind. If she was too rough or pulled his tail, he simply retired to the hole in his kitty condo.

Ramona, who had hoped someone would go with her to the park so she could work on a new set of calluses, now felt her life was full of chores. She washed Clawed's dish, changed his water even though he drank from the toilet, served his meals, brushed his hair off the couch, brushed Clawed himself so he wouldn't shed so much, watched him when Roberta was crawling around on the floor. She began to look forward to Clawed's going home.

Then late one afternoon when Beezus was at Abby's house and Ramona was sitting on the floor keeping one eye on Roberta and Clawed and her other eye on a book, Mrs. Quimby said, "Do you think you could watch Roberta while I drive over and pick up Beezus? I'll only be gone a few minutes."

"Sure, Mom." Ramona felt a ripple of pleasure. She had been promoted from cat-sitter to baby-sitter. She was proud that her mother finally trusted her.

"You're sure?" asked Mrs. Quimby.

"Of course I'm sure. I watch her all the time," said Ramona, and added words she had heard Beezus speak so often. "Mom, you worry too much."

"That's what mothers are for," said Mrs. Quimby as she went out the door.

"Now, you be a good girl," Ramona instructed her baby sister, who was sitting on the floor holding her precious little blanket against her face.

Roberta looked agreeable to being a good girl. She pulled a magazine off the coffee table, tearing the cover off as it fell to the carpet. "E-e-e," squealed Roberta, so delighted with her accomplishment she dropped her blanket. With both hands she rumpled a few pages, a sound that disturbed Clawed, who was napping under the window.

"No-no, Roberta," said Ramona. "Don't hurt the nice magazine."

Roberta had seen her mother leave. She gave Ramona a you're-not-my-mother-and-I'm-not-going-to-stop look and rumpled a few more pages. She did not intend to mind her sister, not when she had invented a new game. She tore off another page and took a bite.

"No-no, Roberta," cried Ramona. "Icky. Nasty. 'Pit it in Ramona's hand."

Roberta's game was getting better. She opened her mouth and let soggy paper fall into Ramona's hand.

"Ick," said Ramona. "Good girl." She pulled the magazine away from Roberta and tossed it on the coffee table. Then she threw the wet, chewed-up paper into the cold fireplace.

While Ramona was doing this, Clawed began to cough, a hacking, gagging cough. Hair balls, thought Ramona, stricken. She hadn't brushed him enough. He was going to throw up, right there on the carpet, and she would have to clean it up. Ugh. Ick. Clawed hacked harder. There was the ripping sound of Roberta tearing up more paper. She had managed to pull the magazine off the coffee table again. At least tearing up a magazine would keep her busy for a while.

"Hang on, Clawed," cried Ramona as she opened the front door. She seized the cat around his heaving middle and, in spite of his weight, managed to carry him outside, down the steps, and set him on the shaggy winter grass. She started back to Roberta. But what if Clawed ran off? What would she do if she lost Jeremy's cat? She decided that Roberta, busy with the magazine, was safe for a few seconds. She returned to Clawed, hung on to him to make sure he wouldn't get away, and ordered, "Spit it out, Clawed," while she worried about what her mother and Beezus—they were due any minute—would say if they found her outside with the cat instead of inside with Roberta.

With one last cough Clawed freed himself of the hair ball.

"Thanks," muttered Ramona as she started to lug him into the house. Clawed had a different idea. He struggled out of her grasp and ran back into the house without any help from her. "Stupid cat," said Ramona. "If you didn't wash so much, you wouldn't get hair balls." She found Clawed sitting on the carpet washing just as Roberta, leaving her blanket behind, crawled toward his uninhabited kitty condo. Before Ramona could reach her, she stuck her head inside the lower hole to see what was inside.

"Roberta!" cried Ramona. What if her mother and Beezus walked in now?

Roberta sneezed and began to cry. The inside of the kitty condo was dark, scary, and full of cat hair. She did not like it one bit. Ramona grasped her little sister around the waist and pulled. Roberta, frightened at being tugged, screamed harder. Clawed stopped washing long enough to look over his shoulder with disapproval. Clawed did not care for noise.

"It's all right, Roberta." Ramona tried to sound soothing as she pulled. Roberta screamed harder, her cries muffled by the walls of the scratching post. Ramona held her breath when she heard a car and let it out when the car did not turn into the Quimbys' driveway. She did not want her mother and Beezus to find Roberta breathing cat hair with her head stuck in a hole.

What do I do now? Ramona thought desperately as she gently stroked Roberta's back to calm her. "There, there. Ramona will get you out." But how? Screaming, Roberta frantically beat her little feet on the carpet and pushed at the scratching post with her hands.

What if she smothers? thought equally frantic Ramona. Should I call 911? Firemen would come and save her, wouldn't they? They often saved people on television. She started for the telephone. But she isn't going to smother, Ramona suddenly realized, not if she's screaming. She has to breathe to scream, and she must be breathing hard from all the noise she's making. Once more Clawed paused in his washing to disapprove. A cat needed peace and quiet, especially when his fur had been rumpled.

I've got to think, Ramona told herself. Fast, before Mother comes home. If Roberta's head went into the hole, it should come out. What was different? Roberta was not crying when she stuck her head in the hole—that was what was different.

Her mouth was closed. Now it was open. Her chin was in the way. All Ramona had to do was get Roberta to stop crying. How? Then Ramona had an inspiration. She said as cheerfully as she could manage when she was so frightened, "Whe-e-ere's Roberta?" Her sister always enjoyed the peekaboo game.

Roberta's answer was to beat her feet harder and go on screaming. Ramona could see her idea was not going to work. She would have to think of something else. She heard another car. Was it? No, it wasn't the Quimby car. She tried to think what else amused Roberta. Then it came to her. Mother Goose rhymes! Ramona gently rubbed her sister's back, put her mouth close to her shoulder, and began softly, "Three little kittens . . ."

Roberta's feet stopped pounding on the carpet. Encouraged, Ramona continued, ". . . lost their mittens . . ." Roberta stopped crying. She must be listening. Ramona went on reciting as she gently tugged at Roberta's shoulders. "Lost your mittens, you naughty kittens! Then you shall have no pie.

Mee-ow, mee-ow . . ." That was Roberta's favorite part of the rhyme. Ramona carefully pulled her sister's head out of the hole and went limp with relief. Then she hugged the baby, who was, at the moment, the most precious person in the whole world. Roberta snuggled against Ramona, who finished the rhyme, "No, you shall have no pie." Roberta was pleased. "Mo-mo," she said.

Ramona kissed her sister. "Mo-mo" was Roberta's way of saying "Ramona." She set Roberta down, handed her the little blanket, ran for a Kleenex, wiped her nose, and threw all the torn pages in the fireplace. Then, as she heard the Quimby car pull into the driveway, she picked up her book. Roberta was holding her blanket against her face with one hand while she sucked the thumb of her other hand and watched Clawed carefully wash the tip of his tail. I did it, thought Ramona. I baby-sat. I was responsible. Worn-out by her responsibility, she opened her book and pretended she had been reading all along, but she was thinking, One more day and Clawed will go home.

"I can see that the three of you got along just fine," commented Mrs. Quimby as she came into the room.

"Yes, and you were gone a long time," answered Ramona.

Mrs. Quimby glanced at her watch. "Only fifteen minutes. There was more traffic than I expected."

Only fifteen minutes. It had seemed like hours to Ramona.

"Roberta looks ready for a nap," said Mrs. Quimby as she picked up the baby—"oopsy-daisy"—and carried her off to her room.

Ramona laid down her book and watched Beezus take off her jacket and unwind her muffler. "I was just thinking . . ." she said, and paused.

"Good for you," said Beezus.

Ramona ignored this and said, "I was just thinking—how do you get to be a cheerleader?"

✦ 10 ✦
The Valentine Box

Early in February the weather changed to wind and snow. Mrs. Pitt managed to shovel a path on the sidewalk in front of her house. Then schools were closed for almost a week. Ramona and Daisy were too busy coasting on the Thirty-seventh Street hill on Mr. Quimby's old sled, "a real antique," Beezus called it, to think about anything that had happened at school.

That was why Ramona was surprised when school reopened and gray envelopes of class pictures were handed out. Feeling sure that Bill had snapped her picture a second before she made a face, she opened her envelope expecting to see herself cute and perky, maybe a little bit pretty. But no. She wasn't cute. She wasn't perky or the least bit pretty. She was a plain, ordinary girl making an ugly face. Ashamed, she shoved her envelope into her book bag.

Unfortunately, everyone in the class had, in addition to a big picture and several smaller pictures, a sheet of pictures of each member shown slightly larger than a postage stamp. Everyone pointed to Ramona's picture and snickered.

Susan said much too nicely, "It's too bad about your picture, Ramona."

Daisy, who was always kind, said, "Don't worry about it, Ramona. We all know you don't really look like that."

Yard Ape was silent. Ramona was suddenly cross with him for not paying attention to her, not even on the bus. It wasn't her fault Mrs. Meacham confiscated his note and embarrassed him in front of the class.

Ramona tossed her hair to show her class she didn't care what they thought. When she returned home that day, she hid her pictures and hoped her family would never find them.

This lasted for about a week until one evening at dinner Mrs. Quimby asked, "Ramona, what happened to your school pictures? Howie's grandmother says he has his." There were no secrets in this neighborhood.

Ramona took a big bite of potato. She wasn't supposed to talk with her mouth full.

"You don't like your picture," guessed Beezus.

Ramona chewed her potato more than potato needed to be chewed.

"Come on, Ramona," said her father. "We love you no matter how you look. Go get them."

Ramona swallowed, sighed, and fetched the gray envelope, which she thrust at her father. He pulled out the individual pictures and passed them around to the family, who, as Ramona expected, laughed. She put on her you-hurt-my-feelings expression and said, "You're being horrid to me."

"I think this is a great picture." Mr. Quimby smiled at his middle daughter. "It captures the real Ramona."

"It does not!" contradicted Ramona.

"Your Grandpa Day is going to love this," said Mrs. Quimby, "and so will your Aunt Bea."

"Mom, that's *mean*! That picture is awful. I hate it." Ramona wondered if this was all worth a tantrum and decided it wasn't. Maybe she was outgrowing tantrums. Instead she explained about Roberta and the peas. She concluded with, "If Roberta had eaten her peas, I would have had a nice picture. At least I don't spit on the floor like Roberta."

Mrs. Quimby reached over and patted Ramona's hand. "We all know you are nicer than your picture," she said.

"Except sometimes," said Beezus.

Ramona ignored her sister. "All the kids at school except Daisy laughed at me," she went on, "and now our relatives will, too." She was beginning to run out of reasons to feel sorry for herself.

Beezus spoke up. "What difference does it make? When we take our family picture for our next Christmas card, you can smile twice as hard to make up for your school picture."

This led to a discussion of how the family should pose for their Christmas-card picture even though Christmas was months away. After that no more was said about Ramona's picture. At school everyone seemed to have forgotten it, too, perhaps because Mrs. Meacham brought out a box decorated with hearts that Ramona could see had been used in the many classes Mrs. Meacham had taught in years past. Mrs. Meacham made a little speech about not hurting anyone's feelings. Everyone must give a valentine to everyone else in the class. Ramona had heard this speech from previous teachers and knew the problem could be solved by buying kits that held enough valentines for an entire class, silly valentines with words such as "Bee my valentine" with a picture of a bee, or "I choo-choose you for my valentine" with a bear driving a locomotive. For special friends some people might enclose a candy heart with "Be my valentine" or "I love you" printed on it. For extra-special friends fourth graders, usually girls, made valentines decorated with heart stickers and paper lace. This was the part of Valentine's Day Ramona liked best.

That week after dinner Ramona worked on her valentines. Of course she made Daisy's first, with a big pink heart surrounded by yellow daisies, which she drew with the colored pencils her father had bought her. She made another with pink and red hearts for Janet and another, a plain valentine with just one heart, for Howie. It looked too plain, so she drew a hammer, a saw, and some nails around the heart. Howie would like that.

The evening before Valentine's Day she addressed her store-bought valentines, leaving Yard Ape to the last because she wasn't sure she should even give him one, no matter what Mrs. Meacham said. Then she discovered she had no more valentines left. Would Mrs. Meacham notice if she skipped Yard Ape? Yes. Mrs. Meacham never missed a thing. Eagle-eyed Mrs. Meacham might even stay after school, open the box, and go through the valentines to make sure everyone remembered everyone else.

Ramona tapped her nose with her red pencil while she tried to think. Roses are red, violets blue—no, that wouldn't do. Everyone said that. Roses are pink, you sti— No. She was cross with Yard Ape but not that cross.

"Bedtime, Ramona," said Mr. Quimby.

The third time her father spoke to her, Ramona was still trying to think of a valentine for Yard Ape, something not too icky-sweet but not really mean. She found Beezus propped up on her bed studying. Ramona sat down on her bed, kicked off her shoes, and began to pull off her socks by the toes. She sighed noisily to get her sister's attention, which was not the same as interrupting her when she was studying.

Beezus looked up from her book. "Something bothering you?" she asked.

Ramona explained her dilemma, which Beezus

did not see as a problem. "Just give him one of your school pictures with the funny face you made. That way he won't know if you gave it to him because you like him or because you don't like him."

Sensible Beezus. Ramona wished she had thought of this herself. She found a picture, stuffed it in an envelope, printed DANNY on the front, brushed her teeth, and went to bed hoping the class would have chocolate-chip cookies at the Valentine's Day party the next day.

The next afternoon, after the bell rang for the last period, the room mother of Mrs. Meacham's class arrived with a tray of cookies (peanut-butter, Ramona's next-to-favorite) and cartons of pink punch. Mrs. Meacham opened the valentine box and asked the valentine monitors to distribute the envelopes.

As Ramona ate her cookies, she sorted through her valentines. Several looked interesting and a couple were lumpy, which meant they had candy hearts inside. Then she found the one she had been looking for, an envelope addressed in Yard

Ape's uphill scrawl. She felt uneasy. Had she made a mistake in giving him her picture? She bit into a cookie and glanced across the aisle in time to see Yard Ape pull her photograph out of the envelope. She stopped chewing. He looked at her picture, grinned, and put the picture in his shirt pocket.

Ramona quickly looked away and tore open his envelope. She pulled out, not a valentine, but a sheet of tablet paper without a single heart. Printed in big letters that ignored lines were the words:

IF YOU ARE EATING PEAS
THINK OF ME BEFORE YOU SNEEZE.
Signed,
Yard Ape
PRESIDENT

An original poem! A poem Mrs. Meacham didn't have a chance to read. Ramona looked at Yard Ape and smiled. He smiled back. Then she carefully folded his valentine smaller and smaller until it was small enough to fit into the little box in which she kept her baby teeth at home. She would keep it forever.

✦ 11 ✦
Birthday Girl

Spring finally came. Rain no longer fell every day. Lawn mowers whirred through the shaggy winter grass. People went to the park again. Everyone, especially Ramona, felt good. One evening, late in May, the Quimby family was enjoying an unusually quiet dinner. The telephone did not ring. Roberta had been fed and, worn-out from pulling herself to her feet by hanging on to chairs, was asleep. Beezus and her father were talking about something—Ramona wasn't paying attention because she was busy examining the new calluses beginning to form on the palms of her hands. The girls at school, those who enjoyed swinging on the rings, were once more comparing calluses. This thought gave Ramona an idea.

"You know what I would like to do on my birthday?" she asked, and did not wait for an answer. "Have a birthday party in the park. We can play on the rings and skip playing pin-the-tail-on-the-donkey and all those babyish games."

"I think we can manage that if Beezus will help with Roberta," agreed Mrs. Quimby, and added, "If it doesn't rain."

"Sure. I'll help," said Beezus. "The park is a good idea. That way the house doesn't get messed up."

Although she knew what Beezus said was true, Ramona ignored her sister and said dreamily, "Just think. I'll be a teenager."

"Aren't you getting ahead of yourself?" asked Mr. Quimby.

"No, you won't," said Beezus. "You will be ten years old."

"That's a teenager, sort of," said Ramona.

"Zeroteen. That's a double-digit number." *Double-digit* sounded serious and important. "And next year I'll be oneteen and the year after twoteen, then thirteen and fourteen." Her family looked amused, but Ramona did not care. She was too busy with her plans. "And I don't want a birthday cake," she continued. "I want a big bowl of whipped cream." Ramona liked thick, soft, fluffy, sweet whipped cream much more than she liked cake, which was sometimes dry and with thin frosting.

"Think of the calories," said Mrs. Quimby, who thought a lot about calories since Roberta was born.

"And the cholesterol," said Mr. Quimby, who sometimes said he should begin to watch his diet.

"Whipped cream will make your face break out in spots," said Beezus, who spent a lot of time looking at herself in the mirror.

Ramona considered all these worries ridiculous, so she ignored them. She leaned back in her chair, closed her eyes, and thought of a big bowl of whipped cream. On a table in the park. Surrounded by birthday presents. With the sun shining through the fir trees.

"But where would you put the candles?" asked Beezus.

Ramona opened her eyes. She had forgotten about candles. "Just—stick them around in the whipped cream" was the best answer she could come up with.

Of course Beezus found something wrong with this. "If you blow hard enough to blow out the candles, whipped cream will fly all over the place."

Ramona was silent. She liked the picture of whipped cream flying across the table with her friends ducking and squealing, but then she wouldn't get to eat the whipped cream. Beezus was right, which Ramona found a tiny bit annoying.

Mrs. Quimby, sensing trouble, quickly said, "I could bake a cake with whipped cream for frosting."

"Okay," said Ramona. "Chocolate cake and thick whipped cream." That evening she sat at the kitchen table to work on her guest list: three girls who were her good friends, four others who had invited Ramona to their birthday parties. She read her list to her mother.

"What about Susan?" asked Mrs. Quimby. "You went to her birthday party."

Ramona made a face. "Yes, but I didn't have a good time."

"That has nothing to do with it," said Mrs. Quimby. "And I think it is time you and Susan learned to get along."

Reluctantly, in less than perfect cursive, Ramona added Susan's name to her list. She did try, medium hard, to get along with Susan, who always waved around her papers on which Mrs. Meacham had written Excellent! Good Work! or Prize Speller! at the top. She hoped Susan would not come. She did not want to hear her mother tell her to play nicely with Susan or her father tell her to cut out this nonsense about Susan.

As it turned out, everyone accepted, even Susan. When Ramona's birthday—the most important day of the year, next to Christmas—finally came, the sky held only a few unimportant clouds. Ramona opened family presents at breakfast. After waffles served with blueberries, Ramona sang, "O frabjous day! Callooh! Callay!"—happy words from a book about a girl named Alice.

Then the telephone rang. Beezus got to it before Ramona. The call turned out to be from a neighbor who had an emergency and needed a baby-sitter right away. "Please, please, Mom, can I take it?" Beezus begged. "These are *nice* people who always have the right change."

"But this is Ramona's birthday," Mrs. Quimby reminded her.

"It's okay with me," said Ramona, who enjoyed having her mother to herself. Along with Roberta, of course. She also liked feeling she was being kind to Beezus.

"Please, Mom," begged Beezus. "I don't want someone else to get their business."

Mrs. Quimby, who was sliding layer cake pans into the oven, reluctantly agreed.

Then telephone calls came for Ramona: Grandpa Day from his mobile home park in California, where he was table-tennis champion; Aunt Bea and Uncle Hobart all the way from Alaska, where Ramona pictured them surrounded by the seals and polar bears she had seen on television. A lovely chocolate smell of baking cake filled the house, and the few clouds in the blue sky remained as fluffy as whipped cream. It was the beginning of a great day.

Finally, *finally,* Roberta was bathed and dressed in her red corduroy overalls. Ramona stuffed her into her little sweater and wondered if she would ever learn to hold her thumbs in so her hands would slip through the sleeves without a struggle. The cake was frosted with swirls of whipped cream, and the car was loaded with the picnic, along with Roberta in her car seat, her diaper bag, and her teddy bear. Ramona buckled her seat belt in happy anticipation. "Whew!" said Mrs. Quimby as she turned the key in the ignition. "We're on our way."

Fortunately, the picnic table Ramona wanted, the one between the wading pool and the playground, was vacant. Mrs. Quimby lifted Roberta out, car seat and all, and set her on the grass where Ramona could keep an eye on her. Roberta waved her hands and feet, fussing, until Ramona released her and, holding her by the hands, helped her walk on the grass. The teeter-totter thumped, rings clanged, little children in the wading pool splashed, tennis balls bounced.

The great day was about to get better. Ramona's guests, all of them carrying interesting packages, came running across the grass. Of course Susan was among them, the only one wearing a dress instead of play clothes. Roberta, crawling fast, started toward the wading pool while the girls piled their presents on a bench. Ramona caught her and brought her back.

"Hello, girls," Mrs. Quimby called out as she laid out plastic forks and spoons on the checkered tablecloth and poured punch into paper cups.

Without a word about Happy Birthday, the

guests hovered over Roberta, cooing, squealing, and admiring. "Look at her tiny fingers with those teeny-weeny fingernails!" "She's so *sweet!*" "I wish I had a baby sister." "Look at her little teeth when she smiles!" Smiling, Roberta crawled away. The girls caught her and brought her back. Roberta had invented a new game that the girls played, catching her and bringing her back.

Ramona felt forgotten. She knew all about Roberta's tiny hands and feet. All babies had them. She knew about her teeth, too. She had listened to Roberta fret and wiped up her drool when she was teething. She marveled at Roberta's growth, but not today. This was her birthday, her very own day, not Roberta's. Ramona sat beside her pile of presents and scowled.

"Ramona!" whispered Mrs. Quimby as she dealt out tuna-fish sandwiches and carrot sticks. "Behave yourself. Smile." Ramona turned up the corners of her mouth, hardly a real smile. Roberta tired of excitement and began to fuss until Mrs. Quimby picked her up.

Ramona's friends then remembered to say Happy Birthday as they gathered around to watch her open her presents. This is more like it, Ramona thought as she untied bows, read cards, and tore fancy wrappings off paperback books, hair bands, stationery, a big box of crayons, and a floppy stuffed frog, while her mother, with Roberta balanced on her hip, poked candles into the whipped cream frosting.

Then, as the girls were eating their sandwiches and carrot sticks, one of them said, "Look! There's Danny!" Everyone looked to see Yard Ape and two other boys climbing up the slides. Ramona knew they felt too old to slide down, so they had to show off by climbing up. "Ee-yew! Boys!" the girls squealed.

On hearing this, Yard Ape and his friends came running and whooping. Ramona's squealing guests all disappeared under the table, hidden by the tablecloth. Roberta howled. Mrs. Quimby tried to comfort her, but she only cried louder, her face puckered, tears streaming down her face.

"Yard Ape, you go away!" ordered Ramona, annoyed at Yard Ape's taking away her birthday. "You're scaring my baby sister." The boys, still whooping, ran back to the playground.

"You can come out now," Ramona ordered her less-than-perfect guests. Roberta stopped howling and looked surprised to see girls crawl out from under the table. She was old enough to know girls did not belong under tables. Mrs. Quimby returned the baby to her car seat on the grass, where, worn-out by excitement, she fell asleep. Somehow, with Ramona helping, Mrs. Quimby managed to serve everyone ice cream, light the candles, and say, "Make a wish." Ramona closed her eyes, unsure of what to wish for. New skates? Susan transferred to another room at school? She settled on an all-purpose wish: I wish all my wishes would come true. Then she blew out all her candles with one breath.

"No cake for me, please," said Susan. "I brought an apple."

The girls looked at her in surprise as she pulled an apple out of her pocket. Not eat birthday cake? Everyone ate birthday cake.

"There might be spit on the cake from blowing out the candles," explained Susan.

Ramona was shocked. "I did *not* spit on my birthday cake," she informed Susan, while her mother continued to serve cake as if nothing terrible had been said.

Susan was very sure of herself. "You could have. Little bits of spit so tiny you couldn't see them." The girls began to giggle. Susan looked superior in that annoying way of hers and said, "My mother says blowing out candles is unsanitary and cake can give you cavities." She crunched into her apple. The girls stopped giggling and looked thoughtfully at their cake.

"You ate cake at other people's birthday parties," said an indignant Ramona. "I saw you."

Susan had an explanation. "Yes, but that was before Mother read a book on how to stay healthy."

Now Daisy spoke up. "I think that's silly. I'm going to eat my cake. I've eaten birthday cake all my life and I'm still alive." Ramona was glad she had Daisy for a best friend.

Susan went on crunching her apple. She frowned. Obviously she did not like to hear her mother and the book called silly.

"All right, girls," said Mrs. Quimby, smiling brightly. "You don't have to eat your cake if you don't want to." Used to Quimby spit, she took a bite of her own cake.

"I hope your apple has a worm in it," Ramona whispered to Susan.

Three girls carefully scraped their whipped cream aside. Two did not touch their cake but ate their ice cream. The rest ate as if nothing had happened. "I think you are all being stupid," Daisy said to the non-eaters. "If you can't see spit, maybe it isn't there."

"You can't see germs, and they can make you sick," someone pointed out. Two girls laid down their plastic forks.

"I don't have germs!" Ramona insisted.

"Of course you do," someone said. "Everyone has germs. You can't see them, but they are there." This set off an argument about germs—how small they were, did they stick together, could they jump.

Even though she suspected her mother of being amused, Ramona spoke sternly to her guests. "You aren't supposed to talk about germs at someone's birthday party."

Daisy spoke up once more. "Who cares about a few teeny germs. It's not like we picked something up off the sidewalk or bit into something someone else was eating."

All the guests except Susan began to eat their cake, which, after all, looked delicious. "So there,

Susan," said one of the girls before she took a big bite.

"See what you're missing," another said. Everyone except Susan agreed that whipped cream was better than frosting. They all wanted whipped cream on their birthday cakes, too.

To everyone's surprise Susan threw her apple across the lawn without even trying to hit the trash can. Her face crumpled as if she were about to burst into tears. Ramona was stunned. People didn't cry at birthday parties unless they were little and missed their mothers. The rest of the girls were shocked into silence.

"Why, Susan." Mrs. Quimby put a comforting arm around her shoulders. "Whatever is the matter, dear?"

"Everything," said Susan through her tears. "Nobody likes me and everybody likes Ramona."

"You are supposed to like people on their birthdays," Ramona tried to explain to make things better.

"I don't mean just on your birthday," said Susan

with a tearful gulp. "I mean every day. People even make valentines for you. All mine were store-bought. You aren't perfect and nobody cares."

Ramona wasn't so sure about the part about nobody caring. Take Mrs. Meacham and spelling—

"I'm supposed to be perfect every single minute," said Susan, her chin quivering.

How awful, thought Ramona, beginning to feel sorry for Susan.

"Nobody's perfect," Mrs. Quimby reminded Susan. "I could tell you a few things about Ramona. Like the time she was playing at Daisy's house—"

"Mother!" cried Ramona. The guests were immediately alert to a dark secret about to be revealed. Having distracted the guests, Mrs. Quimby did not continue.

Susan was too engrossed in her troubles to be curious. She sniffed and said, "Even Yard Ape likes Ramona."

Here Ramona modestly lowered her eyes. Other girls giggled. Mrs. Quimby hugged Susan and said, "Cheer up. Things are often not as bad as they seem."

"That's right," agreed Ramona. "I survived spelling."

These words seemed to comfort Susan.

"Maybe I could eat a little piece of cake," she ventured with a sniff. "I don't think Mother would mind if I don't eat the whipped cream and if I brush my teeth as soon as I get home."

Ramona was relieved that the other girls did not laugh at Susan. It must be terrible, always having to be perfect when everyone else was messy and full of faults part of the time, maybe even most of the time. She discovered she really felt sorry for Susan.

The other girls' attention had been diverted from Susan. "Mrs. Quimby, tell us about what happened when Ramona was playing at Daisy's house," one of the girls requested.

Fortunately, at that moment Roberta woke up, felt wet and neglected, and began to cry. Mrs. Quimby, having comforted Susan, went off to change and soothe Roberta.

Daisy, eager that the question not be answered when Mrs. Quimby returned, said, "Let's see who has the biggest calluses." Hands were held out, calluses felt, and it was agreed that those who lived closest to the park were lucky. Ramona felt secure. By the end of summer she would have super calluses.

Mrs. Quimby finished changing Roberta's diaper and returned to the table with the smiling baby in her arms. Before anyone could ask again what had happened at her house, Daisy spoke up. "Let's go play on the rings."

The girls, even Susan, scrambled from the table, remembered their manners, and chorused, "Thank you for the party," before they ran off to the rings. Mrs. Quimby started to clear the table with her free hand, and even though she wasn't sure a birthday girl should have to clean up after her own party, Ramona felt obliged to help. After all, she lived near the park and would have plenty of time to swing on the rings when school was out.

"You know, Ramona," said Mrs. Quimby, "Susan's mother isn't the only one who has read a book. The book I read said ten is the nicest age of growing up. It said ten-year-olds are pleasant and agreeable."

"That's me," said Ramona, suddenly at her pleasant and agreeable best.

Mrs. Quimby dropped a kiss on Ramona's hair before she changed the subject. "I wonder what we should do with the rest of this cake," she said. "Whipped cream doesn't keep very long."

Ramona saw Yard Ape and his merry band of two running across the grass. "Feed it to the boys," she said to her mother, and called out, "Hey, Yard Ape! Want some birthday cake?"

"Sure." Danny picked up a tennis ball a beginning player had batted over the fence and threw it back. Then he and his friends came running.

Ramona seized the knife and clumsily divided the leftover cake into three pieces. The boys picked up their cake with their fingers and sang, led by Yard Ape, "Happy birthday to you . . . happy birthday, dear Ramona. You belong in a zoo."

Ramona could ignore the part about the zoo because she was secretly pleased that Yard Ape had called her dear Ramona even if the words were part of a song everyone knew.

The boys finished their cake, licked their germy fingers, and wiped them on the seats of their germy pants. "Thank you for the birthday cake," said Yard Ape, who must have been taught manners, even if

they did not show in school. "Happy tenth birthday."

"Zeroteenth," corrected Ramona. "I'm a teenager now."

Yard Ape stopped. "I never thought of it that way." He started off across the grass.

"And I'm a potential grown-up!" Ramona called after him.

"Me too!" Yard Ape shouted back.

"Come on, Ramona," one of the girls called out. "It's your birthday."

"Run along," said Mrs. Quimby as she returned Roberta to her car seat.

"I'm coming," Ramona answered. Her sticky fingers would help keep her hands from sliding off the rings. The sky was blue, little children still laughed and splashed in the wading pool, the rings clanged. She felt better about Susan. Yard Ape liked her. The day was perfect—well, not really, but close enough.